STRANGE THINGS HAPPEN HERE

Stories by Allan Kemp

Contact info

Email: **theallankemp@mail.com**

Twitter: @theallankemp

Website: **http://www.theallankemp.com/home.html**

Illustrator: Erica Petit Illustrations

Cover Model: Maryna Stenko

"The Girl in the Lumpy Sweater" first published in Voluptuous Magazine November 2000.

"The Bra Man Cometh" first published in Score Magazine August 2004.

"Feed the Baby" first published in Summer 2011 Dark Gothic Resurrected Magazine.

"Spikes" first published in Babes and Beasts- Tales of Lusty Shifters by Bloody Kisses Press, June 2015

CONTENTS

FOREVER AND A DAY

The clock on the wall was broken with time frozen at a quarter to twelve. It had never been a functioning timepiece, merely part of Tallulah's carefully designed rustic décor. The bar and grill was only two years old, yet it wanted to project the feeling of a battle-worn neighborhood dive bar. The polished wood tabletops and wide screen televisions tainted the illusion, however the patrons didn't seem to mind. The food was good, the drinks were poured with a heavy hand, and the bartender remembered your name.

Tallulah's was a lesbian bar, though men gay and straight were welcome. Gone were the days when a Y chromosome was treated as an unwanted intruder. But there was something about the man who entered on this late Thursday afternoon that sent a wary shiver down everyone's backs.

He didn't walk in; a mountainous man in a black chauffeur's uniform wheeled him in. Wrinkled, shriveled-up, at death's door, Methuselah's big brother, and older than dirt were among the weak attempts made by the women in the bar to describe how old the man appeared. Instead of the expected nursing home attire, he wore an expensive suit, wraparound sunglasses, and a beret.

Turning his turtle-like neck from side to side, he pointed a boney finger at a booth along the wall, where two women were sharing a bottle of white wine. One was lean with the reddish brown skin, wide cheekbones, dark eyes, and straight black hair of a Native American. The other was of Irish descent, with short red hair and a mass of freckles across her face. They looked to be in their late thirties and both wore dress shirts with the sleeves rolled up and pressed jeans. The chauffeur pushed the wheelchair to their table.

The bar wasn't crowded and there wasn't much on TV, so the old man had everyone's attention except for the two women in the booth. He waited patiently for a break in their conversation. Finally after five slow minutes, they acknowledged his presence.

"*Salut*, Chepi," he said in a low raspy voice.

The Native American rolled her eyes and gave the geezer a fake smile. "*Bonjour*, Jacques. What brings you back to Quebec?"

"I searched all over the world for you. I never would have guessed I would find you here."

"I wanted to return to my people."

"*Merde*! You don't care about the Algonquins. If you did, you never would have left them."

Chepi sipped her wine. "You know why I left."

Jacques pointed a trembling finger at the Irish woman. "Is she a member of your tribe? Or you latest victim?"

Chepi ignored his question. "Well, you found me. What do you want?"

"The only thing I could possibly want from you. Release this curse you put on me."

"Curse? I gave you what you wanted."

Jacques waved at the chauffeur, who leaned down for his instructions. "Brian, go to the bar and get me a glass of water. Then once you've done that, go back to the bar and wait."

Brian lumbered away.

"He's cute," Chepi said. "Do you pay him by the hour or is he salary?"

"You deliberately deceived me," Jacques growled.

"Should I leave you two alone?" asked the Irish woman.

"It's up to you, Kira," said Chepi. "You're welcome to stay as long as you have the stomach for this coffin-dodger's ramblings."

Kira refilled her glass. "Then I'd like to stay. He's very entertaining."

Brian returned with a glass of water.

"Where's the straw?" Jacques asked.

Brian quickly fetched a straw. He peeled off the paper and put the plastic tube into the clear liquid. He held the glass so that the straw was level with Jacques' mouth. Jacques noisily sucked on the straw. Some of the water dribbled out of the side of his mouth and down his chin. Brian took out a handkerchief and dabbed Jacques' chin before leaving the glass on the table and retreating to the bar.

"Like I was saying," Kira said. "He's very entertaining."

Jacques shifted in his wheelchair so that he was facing Kira directly. He removed his sunglasses and glared at her.

"This *putain* you are sleeping with is not what she seems," he said. "She is an evil witch."

Chepi attempted to sip her wine, but the glass was empty. Her hand trembled slightly as she refilled her glass. Beyond the soft folds of skin, she could still see the twinkle in Jacques' watery eyes and a few strands of wavy brown hair stubbornly held on to his bald, liver-spotted head.

"So what exactly did Chepi do to you?" Kira asked. "You said something about a curse?"

"*Oui!* A curse! She stole my youth and trapped me in this decrepit vessel."

Kira recoiled in mock surprise. "Chepi is a succubus?"

Jacques pounded the armrest on his wheelchair with his fist. *"Oui*! A succubus! A demon from hell!"

Kira laughed loudly.

"This is no joke," Jacques said. "She's a witch. I'm proof she's a witch."

Kira stopped laughing abruptly and narrowed her eyes at Jacques.

"You're so full of shite. You've always been full of shite."

Fear seeped into the crevices of Jacques' face. "You talk as if you know me, but I've never met you before. Are you a witch too?"

"Stop playing around. You know I'm a witch. You knew I was a witch the first time we met was in Paris in 1875 back when I dancing at the Moulin Rouge. Even though you knew I was a close friend of Chepi's, you tried to seduce me. I told you to go to hell. You tried again in 1925 in Munich. Again, I told you to go to hell. And then there was that time in London in 1962. I told you to go fuck yourself."

"You're lying. I've never laid eyes on you. You're trying to trick me."

Kira slid out of the booth. She put her hands on the wheelchair's armrests and yanked it toward her. Jacques shrunk back in his seat. Brian hurried over to rescue his employer. Kira waved her hand dismissively at him. The muscle-bound giant's eyes went blank. He stood stiffly at attention then marched back to his seat at the bar.

Kira's face was flushed with anger as she bore down on Jacques. "You don't remember any of the skirts you've chased over the centuries. Once you got what you wanted, you tossed the girls aside along with the memory of their names and faces. I've seen you do it a million times, you fucking shitehawk."

"It's not true," Jacques said. "And even if it was true, I don't remember. My memory isn't what it used to be."

"Don't lie to me," hissed Kira.

She felt a hand on her shoulder. Chepi was standing behind her.

"I believe he's telling the truth," Chepi said. "Human bodies weren't meant to operate as long as his has. Many of his organs have probably atrophied by now. I'm more than a little surprised that he remembers me."

"It's not fair. He should at least remember what he did to you."

Chepi pulled Kira into her arms and hugged her. "Thank you, my love, but I should handle this."

Kira nodded and sauntered to the bar. The after work crowd, eager for a drink and someone to grouse about their day, started to wander in. The smell of fried food and perfume filled the air. Kira sat on a barstool next to dazed Brian.

"You look like you could use a drink," she said. "Goddess knows I do." She motioned for the bartender. "Two shots of Jameson's with water chasers."

At the booth, Chepi gently guided Jacques to her side and sat so that their knees were touching.

"I have forgotten many things," Jacques said, "but not you. I remember everything about you."

She reached out and held his wrinkled hands. "Put aside your anger for a moment so that we can talk."

He felt a tingling pleasure that replaced the arthritic pain in his joints. The tingling raced up his arms and spread throughout his body. His lungs filled and his constant wheezing was banished. He even felt a tingling in his penis, the first time he'd felt any pleasurable sensation in that area for decades.

With his sense of smell rejuvenated, he savored Chepi's scent: a mix of pine, lavender, and fresh clean air.

"I've always loved how you smell," Jacques said. "It brings back not full memories, but snatches of the past. I see you bathing in a waterfall. I smell cigarettes, red wine, and the laughter of good friends. I remember children laughing. Not yours, but mine. I remember those same children on their deathbeds." Jacques squeezed his eyes shut and shook his head. "It's too much. Don't bring back all the memories. They will fill my head until it explodes."

Chepi closed her eyes and squeezed Jacques' hands. "One thing I've never accused you of is cowardice. Be brave. We'll remember together."

#

It was 1610, according to the Christian calendar, when Jacques Fournier came to live with an Algonquin tribe in the territory known as New France. He was a 22-year-old fur trapper eager to make his fortune.

It was common practice for the trappers to join the Indians and to take one of their women as a bride. He chose their medicine woman, Chepi.

"There are more attractive women in our village," the chief told Jacques. "Choose one of them."

"I can't," Jacques said. "There's something mysterious about her smile that I find irresistible."

"She has strange magic. That is why none of the men have chosen her. For your own safety, stay away from her."

"Strange magic. What does that mean?"

The chief wouldn't elaborate. Jacques ignored the chief's warning and courted Chepi. After years of being ignored by all the eligible men in the tribe, she was starved for attention. She fell deeply in love with the tall handsome man with the dancing brown eyes and soft wavy hair.

They made love for the first time under a full moon in the forest next to a waterfall. Shortly afterwards, they married.

Three years later in their hut in the middle of the night, Chepi's sobbing woke Jacques from a deep sleep. She refused to tell him why she was crying. Finally after much coaxing, she confessed that she was not a normal woman.

"I can't bear children."

"That's okay," Jacques said. "Children are noisy and destructive."

"I can't because I'm a witch."

Jacques didn't believe her, so she cast a spell that caused his beard to grow so rapidly that in seconds filled the dirt floor of their hut. Then she cast another spell and his beard was instantly back to its former length. In a blind panic, he stumbled out of the hut and ran into the woods. He returned the next night calmer and with a million questions for his bride. They talked until dawn.

Her immortality was of special interest to him. He imagined the immeasurable wealth he could amass with unlimited time. Another reason she cried herself to sleep was because she couldn't bear the thought of living without him, so he pressed Chepi on whether there was a way she could give him immortality as well.

"Would you be willing to live forever with me?" Chepi asked.

"Of course I would," Jacques said. "I love you. That's why I chose you."

Chepi created a potion from roots and vines she collected from the darkest places in the forest. She added her blood to the potion and had Jacques drink it.

"You will live forever and a day," she said. "And we will stay young together."

They were happy together for many years. However, by the early 1700s, gossip circulated among the tribe that evil spirits had taken possession of them and that was why they never seemed to age. If that weren't enough,
there were frequent skirmishes with the Iroquois, and the fur trade began to decline. Jacques decided it was time to leave the village.

Chepi refused to go. The Algonquin were her chosen people. Jacques gave her an ultimatum--she had to choose either him or the tribe. Chepi chose Jacques.

They moved to Oregon where Jacques got a job with the Hudson's Bay Company. He earned a good salary and invested in emerging businesses including the railroad. When the 1800s rolled around, he was a wealthy man. Jacques and Chepi left the United States at the start of the Civil War and moved to France.

In the early 1900s, they left France and moved to Switzerland, where Jacques became a banker. The two world wars devastated Europe, but Jacques continued to gather wealth. At the end of World War Two, they traveled the world.

During these centuries, Chepi allowed Jacques to sleep with any woman he chose as long as he returned to her bed afterwards. If one of those women became pregnant, Chepi encouraged Jacques to have a relationship with the child. She did this because she felt guilty for denying him a family.

Their arrangement worked for three hundred and forty seven years. In 1957, they were living in London and Jacques announced that he was leaving Chepi. He was beyond bored with her. She begged him to reconsider, but his mind was made up. He offered her half his fortune, but she refused. She was a witch. She didn't need money. All she ever wanted or needed was him.

Jacques celebrated his freedom with a round the world excursion of bars and brothels. His debauchery ended on a blurry morning in 1968. He stumbled out of bed in his suite in Amsterdam, looked in the mirror, and noticed wrinkles under his eyes. Within a month, his hair turned gray and then fell out in clumps. He wasn't just aging; he was aging rapidly. The years were catching up with him.

He spent millions trying to slow down the process, but to no avail. Doctors were as baffled by his accelerated aging as they were with what was keeping him alive. If his body was as old as the tests indicated, he should have been dead years ago.

Jacques decided that Chepi had cursed him out of spite. He had to find her and force her to give him back his youth. He returned to London in 1980, but she wasn't there.

For the next thirty-five years, he searched the world for Chepi, only to find her in the land where he first laid eyes on her mysterious smile.

\#

Jacques and Chepi opened their eyes.

"You lied to me," Jacques said. "You promised we would stay young. Only you stayed young."

Chepi massaged Jacques' arthritic hands with her smooth fingers.

"I said we would stay young *together*. I didn't create the spell, but the witch who did knew something about lovers. They can't be trusted to love you forever. So the staying young part only works as long as the lover remains with the witch."

The dreadful truth dawned on Jacques.

"The moment I left you, I doomed myself."

"You are 427 years old and no closer to dying than you were the day you were born."

"But I feel every one of those four hundred and twenty-seven years years. How will I feel when I am 527 or 1000?"

Chepi shook her head sadly. "I don't know."

"Please kill me. You have the power to do it. I know you do."

Chepi pressed his hands against her cheek. He could feel her tears.

"Not until you say the words I need to hear from you," she whispered.

Jacques' lower lip quivered as he spoke the words he hadn't spoken in so long. "*Je t'aime.*"

"Don't tell me you love me. That's too cruel. No. Tell me the words I need to hear."

"My pride is too great. I don't know if I can."

"Please, Jacques. Try."

"*Pardonnez-moi*. Please forgive me."

Chepi sighed and put Jacques' hands on his lap. She dug into her purse and took out a small vial containing a greenish-yellow liquid. She poured it into Jacques' water glass, and held the glass up so that the straw was level with his mouth.

"You just happened to have that with you?" Jacques asked.

"I knew you'd find me eventually."

"You said forever and a day. I suppose this is the day."

Chepi nodded. Jacques drank the liquid. A little dribbled out of the side of his mouth and down his chin. Chepi took a napkin and gently dabbed it clean.

CATS AND DOGS

The couple had a deer in the headlights look in their eyes so Dr. Hirsch gave them his most reassuring smile. The marriage counselor's office was designed to put clients at ease. The walls were painted a soothing pale blue and table lamps with off-white shades provided soft lighting. Aquamarine cushions sat in the corners of a beige sofa.

"This is a safe place," Dr. Hirsch said as he gestured for the couple to sit. "There's no judgment here. You're free to be your true self."

Dr. Hirsch sat in his armchair, which was a neutral shade of green. The couple sat at opposite ends of the sofa. The wife pulled the cushion on her side into her lap. Her long fingers kneaded the fabric.

"Do you validate parking?" the husband asked.

Dr. Hirsch smiled tightly. The question was a common delaying tactic used by many new couples.

"Yes, but we'll deal with that at the end of the session."

Dr. Hirsch thought they were attractive, but not in the conventional sense. Both were tall and muscular with sharp cheekbones, but something about their lanky limbs reminded him of a pack of feral dogs he'd seen during a camping trip. The dogs had the familiar features of domestic pets, but the spare mechanics and hungry stare of wild animals.

"So, Bagheera and Akela," Dr. Hirsch said. "Let's get started."

"I don't know where to begin," the wife said.

"Wait a minute. Bagheera and Akela. I knew those names sounded familiar. They're characters from 'The Jungle Book.'"

The wife smiled. "That's right. When Akela and I first met, we realized that his parents and my parents had both loved the book. Seemed like destiny that we would end up together."

"I loved those books too. Much better than the Disney movies."

"Totally. The movies were too sanitized."

"I've never read the books," Akela said, "or seen the movies."

Bagheera sighed and continued to knead the cushion in her lap. Akela scratched behind his ear.

"I really meant it when I said that this is a safe room," Dr. Hirsch said. "You can be yourself here. You can let it all hang out."

Akela and Bagheera looked at each other nervously.

"Are you sure about that?" Akela said. "I don't think you understand what you're suggesting."

Dr. Hirsch leaned back and crossed his legs.

"I've been counseling couples for many years now. You wouldn't believe what I've seen and heard. But in the end, the couples always end up having a better understanding of each other and their relationship is stronger."

Bagheera and Akela looked at each other. She shrugged and he nodded. The couple stood and began to remove their clothing. Dr. Hirsch had never had this happen before. He tried to hide his surprise and failed miserably. Their bodies were well conditioned and their skin was deeply tanned. Once nude, they carefully folded their clothes and stacked them in a neat pile on the armrest of the sofa.

"Well, I did say to let it out hang out," Dr. Hirsch said with an awkward laugh. "I hope you don't mind if I keep my clothes on."

They didn't answer. They closed their eyes and their brows wrinkled with concentration. The sickening sound of bones cracking and muscles expanding filled the room as their bodies contorted and fur sprouted over arms, legs, bellies, and backs. They increased in size and girth. Their faces stretched into snouts. They opened their mouths, exposing rows of sharp teeth.

Paralyzed with fear, Dr. Hirsch remained in his seat even though his brain begged him to run screaming from the room.

When the transformation was complete, Akela and Bagheera opened their eyes. Their eyes were no longer human, but the eyes of beasts.

"We tried to warn you," Bagheera said in a deeper voice than the one she came in with.

She and Akela sat on the sofa and it groaned from the excessive weight. Dr. Hirsch worried that it might collapse at any moment, but then realized that a broken sofa was the least of his worries.

He kept an emergency Xanax in his shirt pocket in case a spouse freaked out during a session. He fumbled for the pill and swallowed it.

"You said this was a safe room where we could be our true selves," Akela said.

"You're werewolves," Dr. Hirsch squeaked.

"Well, Akela is a werewolf," Bagheera said, pointing at her spouse. "I'm a werepanther. We're both shapeshifters."

Dr. Hirsch forced himself to calm down enough to see the difference. Bagheera had the smooth black fur, emerald eyes, and feline jaw of a panther, while Akela had the shaggy fur and canine features of a wolf.

"You really are characters from 'The Jungle Book.'"

"Does that make you Mowgli?" asked Bagheera.

Dr. Hirsch wasn't sure if it was the Xanax kicking in or the fact that the couple hadn't tried to kill him, but he began to relax. He accepted the surreal situation he found himself in and his professional training kicked in.

"Now that you're comfortable," he said, "maybe we can begin to explore what's gone amiss in your marriage."

"She's a panther and I'm a wolf," Akela said. "What else do you need to know?"

"My mother warned me that we'd end up fighting like cats and dogs," Bagheera said. "I didn't want to listen, but she was right."

Bagheera kneaded the cushion. Dr. Hirsch cringed as her sharp talons reduced it to a handful of stuffing.

"Fight like cats and dogs," Dr. Hirsch said. "Let's go with that. How exactly do you fight like cats and dogs? Do you hiss and growl at each other?"

Akela's lip curled back to show his fangs.

"That's a stereotype," he said. "We argue like normal couples. It has more to do with what we argue about. She gets mad when I hang out with my pack. I'm a pack animal. It's what we do."

"All his pack does is chase pretty girls and howl at the moon," Bagheera said. "While I sit at home by myself."

"At least I'm doing something fun. When you're not grooming yourself, you're taking a nap."

Bagheera hissed at Akela and he growled back at her.

"Okay, we've covered some of the issues that drive you apart," Dr. Hirsch said. "What was it that brought you two together in the first place?"

Akela scratched his chin and wagged his tail. Bagheera narrowed her eyes and purred.

"We met at Hooters," Akela said. "I was there with my pack and she was our waitress."

"He was the only one at his table to leave a tip," Bagheera said."

"It was love at first sight."

Bagheera's tail flipped back and forth.

"How is your sex life?" Dr. Hirsch said.

"Despite the arguing, we still mate on a regular basis," Akela said. "Animal sex is always good."

"I have to agree with that," Bagheera said. "What it lacks in the romance department, it more than makes up in the scratching that deep itch department."

Dr. Hirsch sank back in his chair and massaged his chin.

"Maybe all your marriage needs is more activities other than sex the two of you can do together."

"What kind of activities?" Bagheera said.

"There must be something you both enjoy doing that you could do together. Maybe you could take a cooking class together?"

Akela bared his fangs again. Bagheera reached over and scratched behind his ears. He calmed down.

"We're on a raw food diet so a cooking class isn't for us," she said.

"There must be something you both enjoy doing that you're not presently doing together."

"Hunting," Akela said. "We both enjoy hunting."

Bagheera growled at Akela. He cowered and his ears flattened beside his head.

"I think we're on to something here," Dr. Hirsch said excitedly. "Why don't you hunt together?"

"Panthers hunt alone," Bagheera said.

"And wolves hunt in packs," Akela said.

Dr. Hirsch leaned so far forward he almost slid to his knees.

"That may be how you're supposed to hunt, but who says you can't change the rules? The rules say cats and dogs can't fall in love, but here you are."

Akela reached across the sofa and rubbed Bagheera's neck. She closed her eyes and purred.

"I'm willing to try anything to save our marriage," Akela said.

"Me too," Bagheera said.

They stood up and walked to opposite ends of the room. Bagheera went the door and sniffed. Akela went to the window and stared at the parking lot.

Dr. Hirsch checked his watch.

"The session is almost over," he said. "I think we've made great progress considering this is your first time. I think you both have a lot to think about before we met next week."

The couple ignored him. Bagheera joined Akela at the window.

"It's the end of the work day," Bagheera said. "Most of the offices are empty."

"There are only a few cars," Akela said, pointing at the parking lot. "I don't think anybody hangs around this part of town after work."

They turned to Dr. Hirsch.

"We're going to try your suggestion," Bagheera said. "And since it was your idea, we're going to give you a fifteen minute head start."

"Only fifteen minutes?" Akela said. "Where's the sport in that?"

"You're right, dear. Make it thirty minutes."

Dr. Hirsch felt like he'd been doused with a bucket of ice water.

"Head start?" he said. "You can't mean what I think you mean. I'm your marriage counselor. You need me. Alive!"

"But you suggested we hunt together," Bagheera said. "When we hunt, we hunt humans."

"What did you think we hunted?" Akela asked.

"But this is a safe room!" Dr. Hirsch said. "You can't kill me in my safe room."

"We have no intention of killing you here," Bagheera said.

"It wouldn't be hunting," Akela said. "And it wouldn't be any fun."

"Now you can leave on your own or we can toss you out the window."

The fear that had paralyzed Dr. Hirsch earlier had the opposite affect now. He bolted out of his chair and through his office door.

"Help!" he screamed as he ran down the hallway. "Help! Somebody's trying to kill me!"

He punched the button for the elevator repeatedly, but nothing happened. He looked back at his office. The door was open and he thought he could see a dark shape in the doorway. He gave up on the elevator and raced down the three flights of stairs to the bottom floor.

He flew out of his office building. Except for a few cars, the parking lot was deserted. He was relived that his car was parked in his reserved space near the entrance. As he fumbled with his car key, he realized that all his tires were flat. They had been ripped to shreds.

Dr. Hirsch scanned the lot frantically, but spotted no one. He looked up at his office window on the third floor. The window was open and a breeze caused the curtains to sway.

He took out his cell phone and dialed 911. He hurried across the lot and was on the sidewalk by the time operator answered.

"911. What's the emergency?"

"I'm on Oak Street, heading toward Tenth Avenue. I need help immediately. They're trying to kill me."

"Who is trying to kill you? Can you describe them?"

"Yes. The husband is seven feet tall with brown and grey fur. He has a wolf's head and tail but he walks upright like a man. The wife is the same height. She has black fur and a panther's head. She also walks like a man. Or a woman. Well, a human. You know what I mean. Please hurry. They're going to hunt me down and kill me."

"Sir. This line is for real emergencies. We don't have time for silly prank calls."

Dr. Hirsch banged on the door of each shop he passed, but they were all closed with the lights turned off. He kicked himself for setting up his office in a sparsely populated part of town just because the rents were cheaper.

"This is a real emergency. They're after me. They slashed the tires on my car."

"Why did they slash your tires?"

"To make it easier to hunt me, of course!"

"Why are they hunting you?"

"Because I'm their marriage counselor."

"Then you must not be very good at your job. Please sir, don't call back unless you have a real emergency."

The operator hung up.

Dr. Hirsch ran two blocks and ducked into an alley. He could feel his heart beating in his chest. He checked his watch. He wasn't completely sure, but he thought more than thirty minutes had passed since he left his office.

He shut his eyes tightly and waited for the death blow he was sure was coming at any second.

Nothing happened. Maybe they were just teasing him and the three of them would laugh about it at next week's session.

Right. And insurance companies will start covering all types of couples' therapy. He dialed 911 again. As he raised the phone to his ear, a heavy weight knocked him to the ground. Bagheera had tackled him. She straddled his torso.

"You're not making this much of a challenge, Dr. Hirsch," she said.

In a blind panic, he struck her with both fists. Caught off-guard, she rolled off of him. He scrambled to his feet and ran.

He left the alley and ran down the street. He could see people on the next block and headed toward them. He shouted and waved his hands, but no one noticed him.

Bagheera leaped over him and landed facing him.

"Booga! Booga!" she shouted.

Dr. Hirsch yelped and hurried in the opposite direction. He ran without thinking about where he was going as long as it was away from her. He looked over his shoulder but she wasn't there. He turned back and she was in front of him again. He had to slam to a halt to keep from running into her. He backed up quickly.

"Meow!" she said.

She swiped at him, but she misjudged the distance and her large paw just missed tearing his face off.

He changed directions again. He sprinted for blocks until exhausted, he stopped to catch his breath and get his bearings. He didn't know where he was, only that he was in remote
location and it was getting dark. There were no street lamps, no buildings, no cars, no people, nothing.

He listened and heard only the wind. The near silence was broken by a wolf's howl. The long hungry moan filled him with fear and gave him new strength to run again.

The street was empty. His shoes pounding the pavement echoed off brick walls. A dark figure appeared at the end of the block. Dr. Hirsch could make out Akela's pointed ears on top of the figure's head.

Dr. Hirsch slipped into an alley and hurried toward the other end. But the alley ended at a brick wall. He beat the wall in frustration.

He was trapped.

From out of the shadows, Bagheera and Akela came forward and stood on either side of Dr. Hirsch. They looked magnificent in the moonlight. Akela's clear blue eyes glowed and Bagheera's muscles rippled under his jet-black fur.

"You led me here, didn't you?" Dr. Hirsch said. "The same way a wolf pack leads their prey to slaughter."

"I studied the terrain and made sure Bagheera chased you here," Akela said.

"I could resist toying with you along the way," Bagheera said. "You know how we cats can be."

"You were right, Dr. Hirsch. Hunting together was a great idea."

"We made a great team. I've never felt so close to my mate."

They held hands and looked deeply into each other's eyes.

"You can't kill me," Dr. Hirsch said. "I saved your marriage."

Still holding hands, they moved closer to Dr. Hirsch.

"If we don't complete the hunt, then the entire experience is ruined," Bagheera said.

"It's like sex without the orgasm," Akela said. "You feel cheated."

"But I'm Mowgli!" Dr. Hirsch shouted in desperation. "You can't kill Mowgli!"

"Sorry," Bagheera said. "You're not the little lost boy in this story. In fact, do you know what your name means in German?"

"German? What does that have to do with anything?"

"Hirsch is German for deer."

"You see," Akela said, "you always were the prey."

In unison, they lunged at Dr. Hirsch. He didn't have time to scream before they tore out his throat. They tore him apart and ate their fill of him. After such a delicious hunt, he made a delicious meal.

They stuffed the leftovers into a dumpster, licked the doctor's blood off their fur, and then headed back to the office building for their clothes and their car. When they were a block from their destination, Akela grabbed Bagheera's arm and spun her toward him.

"Damn it!" he said. "I forgot to get the parking ticket validated."

FEED THE BABY

"Kwame, it's Mutt. I need your help. I have to feed a baby and it's got to be tonight."

"Why you calling me? I ain't no stink ass vampire."

"I'll feed the baby, but I need your help getting the food. Come on Kwame. There's no else I can turn to."

"I don't know, Mutt. You're asking a lot."

"Kwame... Shannon is the baby."

"Damn, dog. I'm sorry. Don't worry. I can make this happen. You home with the baby?"

"Yeah."

"Unlock the basement door. I'll see you when I see you."

Feeding a baby was slang for providing the first victim for a freshly made vampire. Newbie vampires were like kittens. They had the instinct for hunting, but they needed an experienced vampire to show them how to properly kill their dinner. I couldn't ask a vampire to bring me a live human, preferably one that wouldn't be missed, so I had to impose on my friend Kwame instead.

I used to hang out with the supernatural. It was fucking awesome. I felt invincible, as if their power rubbed off on me.

One night I was out clubbing and I spotted Shannon on the dance floor. She was so fucking beautiful, and the girl knew how to shake what God had given her. I was hopelessly smitten. None of my usual bullshit worked on her so I whipped out my supernatural card. She was impressed. We dated. It was good. It was better than good. It was the best.

Together, we smoked dope with werewolves, attended vampire drag queen shows, and got drunk with wizards who could turn water into bourbon. We spent many a dawn talking about the amazing sights we'd seen before making love until we passed out from exhaustion.

It was all fun and games until the werewolf rips your face off. That's what almost happened to me. I don't know what I said to piss him off, but the werewolf was on top of me before I realized what was happening. Luckily, Kwame was there to pull him off me.

I learned my lesson. I stopped hanging out with the supernatural. I tried to get Shannon to quit with me, but she was too into it. She called me a coward and a wimp, but mainly, she called it quits.

I hadn't seen or heard from her for months. Not until last night when she appeared naked and covered in blood at my front door.

I went to the bathroom that I had turned into a temporary burial chamber. A blanket draped the only window. Another blanket lined the tub. Wood planks over the tub acted as a crude coffin lid. I bent down and pressed my ear against the two by fours. What did I expect to hear? Snoring? Breathing? You needed living lungs for either and the person inside was no longer alive.

What I heard could be mistaken for a living being. I heard a woman crying.

I removed the planks and gently lifted the blanket. Shannon looked like she had climbed into the tub for a nap. Her pale skin matched her white blonde hair. She tried to smile and failed. Her face was wet with tears. Vampire physiology was such a mystery to me. Where did the tears come from?

"I really fucked up this time, didn't I?" Shannon said. She pushed back her upper lip to show me a long sharp vampire fang. "I'm one of them now."

I wanted to pull her into my arms and tell her that everything was going to be all right, but that was a stupid lie that would only make the next step harder.

Shannon stretched like a cat waking from a nap and the sheet covering her naked body slipped down. I tried not to stare at her soft breasts and dark red nipples.

"How does it feel?" I asked.

"Like I'm not myself," she said.

"You aren't. The Shannon I knew died in my arms last night."

Shannon noticed that her breasts were uncovered. She pulled the sheet over them.

"I'm sorry, but I couldn't think of any other place to go."

"It's okay," I assured her. "I'm glad you came to me. Though, it was quite a shock to find a naked woman covered in blood and God knows what else on my front porch."

Shannon lower lip trembled. Great, she was going to start crying again and it was my fault.

"You tried to warn me," she said. "You said it was like the guy from Siegfried and Roy, whichever one was attacked by his own tiger. He knew there was a chance that someday one of his big cats would turn on him and sure enough, one day a tiger snapped and fucked him up good."

"What the fuck happened?" I asked.

"I was at a vampire party. Everything was cool, but then I ran into Stephen. He asked me about you. He wanted to know why you didn't come around anymore. You used to let him suck your dick and I think he developed feelings for you."

"I only let him do it because blood isn't the only thing vampires are good at sucking."

"Are you asking me to suck your dick?"

"No. I mean, if you really wanted to, maybe, but now's not a good time."

49

"Whatever. Back to last night, I was still pissed off at you, so I told Stephen you didn't have the balls to hang with the supernaturals. He and the other vampires had a good laugh at that and I figured that was the end of it."

The idea of Shannon dissing me in front of a bunch of doucebag vampires stung like hell, but I had to know the rest.

"Obviously, that wasn't the end of it."

"The other vampires were ready to talk about something else, but Stephen wouldn't let it drop," Shannon said. "He went on and on calling you a loser and shit like that and then he said, 'You know what would really be funny? If we turned Mutt's little bitch and then left her on his doorstep. First he'll shit his pants with fear, and then she'll kill him.' I tried to run. Their bites hurt at first, but then I passed out."

This was the main reason why I stopped hanging out with the supernatural. They didn't think like us humans. They weren't burdened by compassion or guilt. They didn't think twice about

50

ending Shannon's life and leaving her to kill me. Maybe Stephen wanted to get back at me for not seeing him anymore, but as for the rest of the vampires this was their idea of humor.

Suddenly, Shannon squeezed my arm. The pain was so intense that tears came to my eyes.

"Let go!" I gasped. "You're crushing my arm."

She released my arm. Regret lined her face.

"Sorry," she said. "Guess I literally don't know my own strength."

Rubbing my arm, I turned to see what had frightened her, half expecting to find Stephen staring at me. Instead, there was a werewolf at the bathroom door. His hairy body filled the doorway.

"Shannon, you remember Kwame," I said.

"Shit, Kwame, I'm sorry," Shannon stammered. "I'm not myself today."

"So I heard," he rumbled, his werewolf voice much deeper than his human voice. "Come downstairs. We're ready."

"Can I put on some clothes first?" she asked.

"How do you feel?" I said.

"Like something inside is trying to dig its way out."

"It's the hunger. We need to feed the baby as soon as possible."

Shannon wrapped the sheet around her body and I held her hand as she stepped out of the tub. We followed Kwame down the steps into the basement. I lived in an old house. The basement had a concrete floor and flooded after big rains.

Two werewolves waited in the basement for us.

"Shannon, this here's my homies, K-Nine Loopy and 3Pig Killah," Kwame said.

"I hear tell you got some nice titties," K-Nine Loopy asked.

Kwame snapped at K-Nine Loopy.

"Why you got to be like that?" Kwame growled. "Show the girl some respect."

"I meant it as a compliment," K-Nine said contritely.

The two werewolves stood on either side of a man strapped to a support pole with duct tape. He had a gag in his mouth. He looked to be around seventeen or eighteen at most. He was handsome with delicate features and the kind of soft lips that teenage girls dream of kissing.

"Who is he?" I asked.

"You really want to know?" 3Pig Killah asked.

"I do," said Shannon. "Especially if he's here for the reason I think he's here."

"He's a Cobb County Christer," Kwame said.

"You know what Cobb stands for, don't you?" said. K-nine Loopy. "Catch One Black Boy. Stupid fucking rednecks."

"This ain't the time and place," Kwame said. "He was part of a hunting party in our neighborhood. Mutt called at a good time. Otherwise, this one would be as dead as his buddies."

Officially, Atlanta didn't have supernatural beings. Plenty of people knew the city's diverse population included vampires, werewolves, witches, and wizards. People like the police department, underground scenesters like myself, and radical religious groups like the Cobb County Christers, also known as the CCC.

The CCC arranged late night werewolf hunting parties. Most of the Atlanta werewolves were African American. A majority of the CCC was white. They often ended up killing as many humans as they did werewolves. I once heard CCC member say, "Kill as many black boys as you can and let Jesus sort out which ones are werewolves."

I moved in close to Christer in my basement and took the gag out of his mouth. He screamed for help. I waited for him to get the fear and desperation out of his system. Finally, I'd heard enough.

"Hey, shit for brains!" I said. "You can holler all night and nobody's going to come rescue you. In this neighborhood, hearing loud strange noises is pretty common. My neighbors will think I'm having a party."

"Oh sweet Jesus, please don't kill me," he blubbered. "I didn't even want to come, but I had to. I don't hate anybody. I really don't. I pray for your kind. I really do."

"What's your name?" I said.

"Dustin," he said. "My name's Dustin."

"So if you didn't want to hunt werewolves, then why did you?"

"It's a rite of passage for all the men in our church. To show that we're God's servants, willing to strike down the wicked in his name."

"And you believe that? That they are the wicked who have to be struck down like animals?"

The werewolves started growling. I knew I shouldn't stir them up, but CCC's self- righteousness really pissed me off. Dustin sensed the werewolves' anger. He didn't want to stir them up either.

"If I didn't come, I'd never be able to live it down. You can get your ass kicked good if you don't join the hunting parties," Dustin explained.

"Yeah, peer pressure's a bitch. Sorry about this, Dustin, but baby's hungry."

I turned around and couldn't see Shannon. I found her hiding in a corner with her back against the dank cement wall. I took her hand and led her to Dustin.

"If you don't feed soon," I said firmly, "the hunger will take over and you'll attack whichever warm-blooded creature is closest to you. That includes me."

"I can't," she whispered. "I don't know how."

Once, a long time ago, I was with a group of vampires when they were mentoring a newbie. I was young and had no business being there, but I wanted to see and experience everything the supernatural world had to offer. The vampires cornered a homeless man in Piedmont Park and coached the newbie through his first feeding. It wasn't until later that I realized how lucky I was that the vampires didn't choose me as the newbie's first meal. I watched the whole thing and afterwards, I went behind a tree and puked my guts out.

Dustin squirmed against the duct tape, but it held him too well. I had Shannon face him, but she held her head down so she wouldn't have to look into his eyes.

I spoke softly in Shannon's ear. "Let your senses take over. Hear the blood pumping through his veins. It's a drumbeat demanding you to listen. Can't you smell it? It tickles your nose and sends shivers down your throat. Taste the sweetness of his life. It calls out to you. Feel the hunger building inside your belly and spreading out to the rest of your body. Give in to your desire to feast on his rich red blood."

Shannon's lips parted and her eyes lowered to half-mast. She swayed as if she were drunk. She unwrapped the sheet from her body and let it slide to the concrete floor. Despite his predicament, Dustin stared at Shannon's naked body from her full breasts to the soft patch of blond pubic hair that covered her pussy.

Her nipples hardened. Her cheeks turned pink. She opened her mouth and her fangs extended like twin erections. The gray in her eyes turned red.

"You're almost there," I said. "Can you feel the change? Doesn't it feel wonderful? Don't hold back. Let it take over."

I glanced around. The werewolves had formed a tight semi-circle around us. Their tongues were hanging out and they were panting. A thin line of drool hung from the corner of K-Nine Loopy's mouth.

Shannon leaned forward and sniffed Dustin's neck. He teeth chattered with fear. Shannon gripped Dustin's shirt and ripped it open. Buttons flew off and plinked on the floor. She hunched over and flicked her tongue over his exposed nipples. He gasped. Her tongue flickered down to his belly button, and then she worked her way up to his earlobes. Dustin struggled to free himself, but he was a fly trapped in a spider's web.

As much as Dustin suffered, my pain was even greater. Shannon teased him the way she used to tease me. Part of me would have traded places with him for one last chance to experience the thrills she gave me.

Shannon tried to look Dustin in the eye, but he shut his eyes tight and turned away. She was not so easily deflected. She unbuckled his belt and pulled down the zipper of his jeans. She slipped her hand under the waistband of his underwear.

"Maybe you don't like me, but he certainly does," she purred.

Shame, wounded feelings, and disgust flickered across Dustin's face. "Yea, though I walk in the valley of the shadow of death, I will fear no evil," he said, meeting Shannon's eyes with fierce determination.

That was his fatal mistake. Not that he was going to survive the night anyway, but never challenge a vampire to a staring contest. That was how they hypnotized you. I hadn't had time to explain the process to Shannon, but she had picked it up naturally. Dustin's expression changed from brave little soldier to horny bastard. Red splotches appeared on his cheeks and neck. Shannon had complete control of him.

Shannon smiled wickedly and yanked his pants down to his ankles. His erect dick twitched with anticipation. I could have cut him loose now, but Shannon seemed to like having him tied up.

She pressed her tits against him, starting at his chest and sliding them down to his crotch.

She cupped each of his testicles in her mouth before putting her lips over the head of his dick.

When Shannon sensed that Dustin couldn't hold back much longer, she pulled his dick out of her mouth. Dustin let out a pathetic sigh. Shannon climbed onto him and wrapped her legs tightly around his waist. With one hand she guided him into her moist pussy. Once she had all of him inside her, the werewolves began to howl.

Shannon rode Dustin hard. She arched her back and tossed her head from side to side. Dustin thrust his hips as best he could from his bound position. She shouted with each slap of skin on skin and he answered with husky

moans. The air was thick with the smell of sex. The werewolves' eyes were glued to every motion.

The knot in my stomach twisted as Shannon moved closer to orgasm and further away from my life.

"I can't hold back any longer!" Dustin shouted.

"Yes! Do it! Do it now!" Shannon answered.

Dustin stood still. The werewolves stopped howling. Seconds dragged by and then Dustin's hips jerked violently. He gritted his teeth and his eyes were closed. Thankfully, his eyes were closed. He never saw Shannon's yawning mouth right before she sank her fangs deep into his neck. He continued to climax as she hungrily sucked the blood out of his veins.

By the time Shannon climbed off of Dustin, he was dead. She grabbed the sheet off the floor and ran upstairs.

"I hope when my time comes, I go like that," K-Nine Loopy said.

"No you don't," Kwame said.

The werewolves used their claws to slice through the duct tape holding Dustin and his lifeless body fell to the floor. They rolled the body into a shower curtain they had brought with them.

"Don't worry about a thing, dog," Kwame said. "We'll take the trash with us on our way out."

"I owe you big time," I said.

"That was one hell of a show," 3Pig Killah said.

3Pig and K-nine left with the body. Kwame hung back.

"So now what?" he asked.

"What do you mean?" I said.

"You feed the baby tonight. What are you going to do when she's hungry tomorrow?"

I stared at the top of the basement stairs.

"I'll worry about that tomorrow," I said.

Kwame nodded his shaggy head.

"Peace and love and all that shit," he said and then he was gone and I was alone in the basement.

I trudged upstairs. I found Shannon back in the bathroom, curled up inside the tub. I squatted down and put my hand on her shoulder. Her skin was cold. There was no human warmth left in her.

"I'm really a vampire, aren't I?" she asked as if there was still some wiggle room on the subject.

"Afraid so," I said.

"Do you know of any other vampires who fuck their victims to death?"

"You're the first one I know of."

"Am I going to do it that way every time?"

"I don't know."

"I really fucked up this time."

"You can stay here. I can make you a real coffin. Something permanent."

"No," she said firmly. "I love you too much to stay."

I wanted to beg her. I wanted to tell her it didn't matter what she had become, she was still the girl I fell in love with. I wanted to tell her I didn't care if she turned on me like Roy's tiger and devoured me.

"Don't worry about me," Shannon said. "I'm not a baby anymore."

THE CULT OF NANCY

"Nolan Smiles. We make it precious," read the words painted on the glass front door.

"Maybe if they weren't so busy making it precious they wouldn't have screwed up," Nancy said under her breath as she propelled herself through the door and into the lobby of the photo studio.

On the walls were the stiff smiling faces of past customers. These markers of family history provided testament to new customers that you could trust Nolan Smiles to make you and yours appear as clean and crisp as a new dollar bill.

Nancy was unmoved by all the pink healthy babies sitting on their mothers' laps next to their proud fathers. The photo she was there to pick up would never find its way into Aunt Julie's photo album or Paw Paw's wallet.

Her business portrait would be properly mounted in a mahogany frame with imitation gold trim. At the base of the frame would be a gold plate with the title "Nancy Twirlly, Southeast District Manager." It would then be hung on the wall of the lobby of Carswell Communications, the best maker of coaxial cables this side of the Mississippi, in the row of upper management portraits.

Nolan Smiles' lobby was filled with parents and children waiting for their chance to sit in front of the camera. Mothers spit-pasted stray locks of hair on their fidgeting children's heads while fathers checked their watches every half-minute. The scent of soap fought the stink of kid sweat and lost. At the front counter, a pimply teenage girl chewed gum and concentrated on an imaginary star in the ceiling.

"Excuse me," Nancy said, impatiently snapping her fingers in the girl's face.

The acne plagued girl broke away from her stargazing to face Nancy.

"Hail Nancy," she said.

"How did you know my name?"

"Excuse me, ma'am?"

"You just said, 'Hello Nancy.' How did you know my name was Nancy?"

"Didn't I wait on you the last time you were here?"

"No, I've never seen you before in my life."

"I help package the photos so I must have seen your name. It happens all the time. I think I met the person, but really I've only seen their picture. Funny how that works, huh?"

"Hilarious," said Nancy returning to the business at hand, "I'm here to pick up my photos and I hope for everyone's sake that they are correct this time."

If the girl noticed Nancy's implied threat, she ignored it, "Yes, ma'am, they're ready. I'll tell Mr. Goodwin you're here."

She picked up the receiver to the phone and pressed a button from a row of buttons on the base. Resting the receiver next to her ear, she smiled vacantly at Nancy. Seconds later, she mumbled into the phone and then hung up.

"He'll be right out with your photos, ma'am."

Feeling moderately relieved that she was at last approaching a resolution, Nancy's mind wandered long enough for her to realize something odd.

"Did you say, 'Hail Nancy' when I first came in?"

The girl studied Nancy's face as if she were expecting it to do tricks.

"Did you just ask me if I said, 'Hell Nancy?'" she asked giggling.

"Never mind," said Nancy, blushing.
She was spared any more interaction with the zit-faced girl because Mr. Goodwin appeared at the counter holding a 9 X 12 envelope. He was rural town handsome, dressed in the prerequisite shopping mall executive outfit of button down shirt, clip-on tie, and pressed khaki slacks. Nancy admonished herself for admiring his curly brown hair, square jaw, blue eyes, and the way he carried his sinewy lanky body in a way that said he would be the perfect companion for a camping trip. What sort of executive was she supposed to be if she let a cute boy distract her with erotic daydreams?

"Ms. Twirlly, here are your photos," he announced gravely, handing her the envelope while keeping steady eye contact. "Let me know which one you want enlarged."

Nancy snatched the envelope from his hand and slipped out the contact sheet inside. She studied the variety of poses she had done at the photo shoot and tried to imagine one of them greeting visitors in the lobby of Carswell Communications.

They were all okay, but just okay. Any one of them would do only what it must do, not what it could have done. What it should have done. Nancy's assessment had nothing to do with vanity. Her looks were best categorized as plain. Normal, everyday plain. She had never felt challenged by this fact and her plainness had actually worked in her favor in business. Ugly women were avoided and beautiful women weren't taken seriously.

The smiling face in the photos was a competent leader, but the smiling face that Nolan Smiles bungled from her first photo session was a leader who inspired. Nancy knew this implicitly even though she had never laid eyes on any of the results of the first session.

On that day, Nancy had been perfect. All her preparations to look her best had been executed without a single flaw. She had made special trips to the hairdresser and the mall to transform herself into the image of the perfect district manager. She had made sure to get a full eight hours of sleep the night before and had arrived at Nolan Smiles a half-hour early.

Most important, she had felt perfect. Her life was on track. She was the master of her destiny.

Then a week later came the awful phone call from Nolan Smiles informing her that the first photo didn't take. Her heart sank right through her office floor. First, they said something in the camera had malfunctioned. Then they claimed that the negative had been accidentally overexposed.

Nancy figured that since they couldn't keep their stories straight that she was obviously dealing with an inept company. She wanted to have the photo redone someplace else. She couldn't understand why Carswell Communications, a company dedicated to cutting edge technology, would use a place like Nolan Smiles that still shot on film instead of using digital cameras.

Nancy was informed that Carswell Communications had an agreement with Nolan Smiles to handle all their photographic needs. Going to another photo studio would make waves. A good district manager, especially a brand new one, didn't make waves.

Despite her misgivings, Nancy smiled bravely through a second Nolan Smiles photo session. She looked the same as the first time,
but the inspiration was missing. She was making do instead of making magic. She just didn't believe that Nolan Smiles could really make it precious.

Precious was a concept that had been missing from Nancy's life for some time. It was one of the things traveling salespeople like Nancy left behind. She believed women who travel for a living leave more behind than men do. Men didn't have to leave their fiancé behind.

Barry had given her a ring and they had made wedding plans, but then she got her dream job at

Carswell Communications. He didn't understand what she found so exciting about eating in greasy spoon diners and driving endless miles of highways to stay in an antiseptic motel room on the edge of a field of weeds.

"Don't you realize how dangerous it is out there?" he asked. "I saw a report on TV just the other night about how women especially have to be careful that criminals don't follow
them to their room and break in. You could end up getting raped or killed or even worse, robbed."

"I admit it's not the safest job in the world," Nancy said. "But I love sales. I promise to take the proper precautions."

"Pete and Lisa invited us over to dinner next Saturday. Are you going to be able to make it?"

"Yes, I'll make it," Nancy said defensively. "Don't give me that look. I'll be back in time."

"Whatever," Barry replied in his best passive aggressive voice, "I can survive without you."

She didn't make it back in time. The manager of the small television station she had gone to see had trouble making up his mind whether to go with

Carswell or a competitor. Nancy stayed over the weekend so she could spend more time convincing him. The extra effort paid off. She got a promotion, but she lost Barry.

She felt anger more than loss. Barry was as competitive in business as she was. Was he so old-fashioned that he couldn't handle a wife as good at her job as he was? Looking back, she had always hated that she could share with him the joy she felt driving alone on a sunny day, singing with the radio, knowing that she was on her way to her next challenge. She had a need to conquer and she wasn't ashamed to admit it. It wasn't an exclusive trait of men.

She also wasn't ashamed to demand that things be done to her liking. Right now, she wanted a photo as good as the one from the first photo session. She wanted a photo that properly represented her new life, her new conquest. She was leaving the road for a corner office. She was going to have her own sales staff reporting from the field. She was going to earn their respect. She was going to do it all and still have time for a life. She was going to have friends, important friends, and who knows she might even get a cat or a male companion.

But this second photo didn't come close to showing Nancy as she wanted to be seen, as she needed to be seen. She couldn't allow it to be the first impression people had of her when they walked into the lobby of Carswell Communications.

"This," she said, her voice starting at a whisper and rising octave by octave to a shriek, "is unacceptable! Unacceptable, unacceptable, un-ac-ceptable!"

Everyone in the lobby stopped what they are doing to stare at Nancy. The parents looked at her in anger and disgust while the children grinned and pointed at the funny crazy lady. The front counter girl's mouth dropped open, allowing her gum to fall out onto the front of her shirt.

"Can we please discuss this in my office, Ms. Twirlly?" Mr. Goodwin asked.

Nancy took a deep breath and gave the room a steely once over. "Sure, your office sounds fine. Let's go."

He led Nancy into a back hallway, past open

studios with cameras resting on tripods in front of carpetcd boxes, to a row of doors. He opened a door and held it for her. Inside was a small windowless room with wood paneling on the walls, a desk that was too big for the room and three chairs, one behind the desk and two in front. It smelled of photographic chemicals. As Nancy settled into one of the chairs in front of the desk, she noticed a nameplate among the order forms and bits of negatives that covered the surface of the desk. It read "Cody Goodwin, Store Manager."

"So, Mr. Cody Goodwin Store Manager, how do you plan to fix the fact that you totally ruined my photo?" Nancy asked before he could get settled in his chair behind the desk.

"We'd be happy to take your picture again, Ms. Twirlly."

"That won't do. It would be just as wrong as this one."

"Well, then what do you suggest?" he asked with the hint of exasperation reserved for impossible clients.

"Give me the first photo! Resurrect the

negative! There must be some kind of advanced photographic doodad that can make it happen."

"Believe me, ma'am. I would if I could," he said with a deep sigh.

Nancy sighed back and tapped her foot. She looked around the room, noticing that there were no photos on the walls or on his desk. Odd that someone working in a photo studio had no photos in his office. Nancy decided it was probably due to his lack of ingenuity.

Her own options were fading fast. What could she hope to accomplish? They weren't going to give her what she wanted. She still couldn't accept that her first photo no longer existed. It was too great a loss.

Since she had taken her demand this far, she wasn't comfortable with walking out with her tail between her legs. She struggled to come up with something she could demand that would make her the winner of this standoff. She needed time to collect her thoughts and devise a plan.

"May I use your restroom?" she asked.

Cody blushed. Under different circumstances, Nancy would have found his embarrassment adorable.

"Yes ma'am. Go to the left and it's the door at the end of the hall."

Nancy left the room quickly. At the end of the hallway, she found two doors, one on each side of the hallway. Neither had a sign indicating what was on the other side. Nancy had no desire to go back and ask which door led to the bathroom. Figuring she had a fifty-fifty chance of being correct, she chose one and entered.

The room was pitch black. She felt along the wall for a light switch, but couldn't find one. Standing still, waiting for her eyes to adjust to the darkness, Nancy heard what sounded like voices far away in a tunnel. It seemed like people singing. Perhaps it was a radio playing. Nancy could dimly make out that she was in a hallway lined with stacks of boxes.

Moving towards the singing voices, she smelled incense. The light grew stronger the closer she came to the singing. Rounding a corner, she stopped abruptly.

The hallway opened up into a large warehouse

filled with boxes. In a far corner, a small group of people huddled in front of a makeshift altar. Candles and long sticks of sweet incense lined the base of the altar. At the center rested an ornate gold frame. Coins and dollar bills lay scattered in front of the frame. Inside the gold frame was a photo of Nancy. The people chanted "All Hail Nancy" over and over again in a deep drone.

Nancy tiptoed closer to the worshippers. Seeing people pray to her photo was a shock, but not as big a shock as the photo they were using for their altar. It was the first photo; the one she was told had been destroyed. Even though she had never seen it before, she knew it had to be the first photo.

She had been right. She was absolutely perfect in the photo. Her hair, her smile, the twinkle in her eye. It was the perfect Nancy.

"This is not the bathroom, Ms. Twirlly," said a voice behind her.

She turned to face Cody Goodwin. The chanting stopped as the people turned to look at Nancy.

"That's my picture!" shouted Nancy. "You lied to me."

"Please, could we discuss this in my office?"

"I want my picture!"

"I promise we will work this out. In my office."

"I don't want to go to your office. I want my picture."

"First give me a chance to explain everything. Let me take you to lunch."

The idea of going to lunch now seemed absurd to Nancy, but what wasn't absurd about this moment? She allowed Cody to lead her away from the altar. She looked back to see the worshippers standing quietly, watching her leave, their faces emotionless.

A short time later, she and Cody were seated in the food court of the shopping mall. She sipped from the straw of an unsweetened ice tea while he took longer drags from the straw of an oversized soda. Watching shoppers calmly go through their normal everyday routines took on an air of the surreal in Nancy's mind after what she had just witnessed in the bowels of Nolan Smiles. How could anything be considered normal after discovering that you were the worshipped object of a cult following?

"So, where do I begin?" said Cody.

Nancy hoped he meant the question to be rhetorical and did not answer.

"There's something special about that photo of you!" he whispered conspiratorially, "It can perform miracles."

"And you know this because…?" Nancy asked.

"It all started when the Keeper of the Negative, that's our photo processor, Judy, felt something divine when she first gazed upon your negative."

"Why art thou suddenly talking with such vast strangeness?" Nancy interrupted.

Cody ignored her and continued, "For reasons that she could not explain, she felt compelled to ask it to grant her relief from the pinkeye she was afflicted with. Can you guess what happened next?"

"The pinkeye miraculously cleared up on its own?"

"Why, yes, that's exactly what happened.

"Please Mr. Goodwin, I didn't just fall off the turnip truck."

"Wait, Ms. Twirlly, that was just the beginning." Cody said, placing his hand over Nancy's.

Nancy was about to pull her hand away, but something stopped her. She studied his face. If she had believed in angels, this is what they would look like.

"Damn, Nancy," she thought to herself, "Why don't you just tear his clothes off and force him to have sex right here on the table!" Out loud, she said, "Okay, Mr. Goodwin, finish your story."

"Well, the sudden pinkeye cure was not enough to qualify in anyone's mind that the photo was divine," Cody continued, "So the Keeper of the Negative approached Our Lady of the Loupe, that's our quality control supervisor, Marcia, and confided in her what had transpired. Our Lady of the Loupe asked the negative to straighten her teeth. Right away she felt a tingling sensation in her mouth and next thing she knew, her teeth were perfectly straight. We have a before and after photo of her back at the store."

"Before and after pictures? Were they taken the moment before and after the miracle? Or did a certain amount of time take place between them? Say, long enough time for 'Our Lady of the Loopy' to have braces on her teeth?"

"The testimony of those who have been touched are all the proof we need."

"Have you been touched?"

"No, I have not. Even though I am the Minister of Nancy, I have not had occasion to ask Nancy to grant me a miracle."

Nancy took a deep breath and tried to fit together what he told her with some kind of logic.

"Let me get this straight. You and who knows how many employees of this particular Nolan Smiles sit around and worship me. You know, you don't treat your God very well. The least you could have done was invite me to some of the services."

"You don't understand, Ms. Twirlly. We don't worship you. We worship this particular photo of you. That is the Nancy who brings us joy and tranquility."

"But it's a photo of me!" protested Nancy.

Cody drummed his finger on the table and looked over Nancy's shoulder as if he recognized someone behind her. Finally, he looked back at her.

"Ms. Twirlly. Are you a Christian?"

Nancy blinked. "Yes, I am. Why do you ask?"

"When you go to church, you read the bible, you face the cross, and you say you're praying to Jesus. But think about it. Jesus died and was reborn thousands of years ago. Until he returns again what you are really praying to is his image. The same is true for the True Believers of Nancy. Or Nancies as we like to refer to ourselves. We pray to the image of Nancy. It is perfect and blessed. You aren't."

Nancy felt a huge sense of loss at what he said. She was surprised at how much it hurt though she wasn't surprised at how familiar the pain felt. She swallowed the lump in her throat and let anger take over.

"Why are you telling me all this?" she demanded.

"I wanted you to understand why I can't give you back your photo."

"At least make one print for me that I can use at Carswell Communications."

"That would be blasphemy!"

"Come on, I'm still the real Nancy. Don't I deserve to have one print of myself, even if I'm not as holy as my photo?"

"Please, Ms Twirlly," Cody pleaded, "We just want to be able to worship in peace without persecution. Giving a non-believer a copy of the photo would go against everything that is holy to us"

"Then let me join. I believe in the photo."

Nancy really she did believe in the photo. Not like Cody Goodwin and the pimple-faced girl, but she did believe. With her belief she felt a stabbing anxiety inside her. She was afraid that maybe the Nancy she aspired to be was stolen from her and preserved in the photo. Like those old superstitions about your soul being stolen by having your picture taken.

"Really Ms. Twirlly," said Cody. "I didn't just fall off the turnip truck either. You won't trick me into giving you a copy of the photo that easily."

Nancy could see she wasn't getting anywhere with Cody. She had only one avenue of action left.

"Well, guess what, you nutroll," Nancy said, spitting out the words, "It's a cruel world. Give me my photo and the 'sacred' negative or I'm calling the authorities."

Cody looked back over Nancy's shoulder and nodded his head. Nancy swiveled around in time to see someone sitting at table at the other side of the food court get up and trot quickly in the direction of Nolan Smiles. Nancy turned back to Cody who was staring at her with a blank expression.

"This isn't over yet," she hissed.

"Yes," Cody said sadly, "I'm afraid it is."

It took Nancy twenty-four precious hours before she was able to cajole the police department into investigating the Nolan Smiles store. When they arrived, they found the doors unlocked and the place empty of human life. It was if nobody had ever worked there. All employees, documents, and photos were missing. Not all the photos. The photos of Nancy from the second photo shoot were on the front counter in the 9 X 12 envelope Cody had given her.

The police scratched their heads and looked in desk drawers and under boxes for a couple of weeks and then filed their results in the unsolved section of their filing cabinets. Nolan Smiles did what any self-respecting corporation would do and blamed Nancy for bullying their employees so badly that they left in protest.

This put Carswell Communication in an odd bind. Nancy had been in pursuit of perfection and pursuing perfection was certainly a goal they endorsed, but not to this extreme. Nancy had to be reprimanded. The corporation didn't feel a dismissal was fair. Instead, they took away her promotion and put her back into the field.

They didn't give her back her old route. They felt it was better to send her out to more remote areas, where news didn't travel as fast.

Nancy was back on the road for a month before it dawned on her that she didn't mind it. She didn't care about her expulsion from company headquarters, either. The promotion, the corner office, and the hope for a normal life were all delusions of happiness. It was out here that she really belonged.

But there was still something missing in her life. She wanted a copy of that photo. Not to pray to or ask for miracles. She wanted that precious evidence that proved for one impossible moment in her life, she had been perfect. That was the miracle she craved.

She was sitting at a window booth in a roadside diner, sipping on a cup of coffee, and watching trucks kick up dust as they drove past when she heard the person behind her whisper the words clearly and distinctly.

"Hail Nancy."

She turned around to see what the person looked like, but there were too many people and they all seemed to be ignoring her. For a moment she thought she recognized the pimple-faced girl who worked the front desk of Nolan Smiles sitting at a booth in the corner. But this girl couldn't have been her. Her skin was too smooth and clean, too free of blemishes.

Nancy didn't mind. She knew she had to be patient. Someday they would let her join them. Until then, she was content in the knowledge that somewhere out there was a miracle with her name on it.

THE ROAD TO HELL IS PAVED WITH GLAZED DOUGHNUTS

Ponce de Leon Avenue is a long winding snake. Its head rests in the heart of downtown Atlanta and its tail slithers to the base of Stone Mountain.

Somewhere along its many coils rests a culinary jewel proudly proclaiming that it possesses "Hot Doughnuts Now." This jewel is a Krispy Kreme Doughnut shop. Their most famous contribution to the world of small oval cakes is the glazed doughnut, a yeast doughnut with a combination of milk and sugar coating on top. It's best served fresh and hot off the long winding conveyor belt that winds throughout the store. A glass window separates the manufacturing of the doughnuts from the front of the store. This way, the customer can be sure that their doughnuts are indeed "hot doughnuts now."

On Tuesday at midnight, there are no hot doughnuts. The conveyor belt is still, and all the unsold doughnuts have been boxed and put away. Tuesday is traditionally a slow night and business dried up around 8:30. The staff locked the doors early at 10:00. By 11:30, they had finished closing down for the night and everyone had gone home except for Mona, a front counter cashier. Once she turns out the lights and sets the alarm, then she'll be gone too.

She emerges from the employee break room where she'd been feeding her nicotine addiction and absently ambles up to the cash register. She's busy seeking out any stray ashes that may have taken refuge on her shirt and doesn't notice the stranger standing on the other side of the counter.

"It's a fine evening for doughnuts, wouldn't you agree?" said the stranger.

The sudden break in silence causes Mona to jump. Clutching her chest to keep her racing heart from escaping, she looks wildly from the stranger to the supposedly locked front door.

"We're closed," she said. "How did you get in here? The door's locked."

"It wasn't locked for me," replies the stranger, his voice as smooth as whiskey soaked in charcoal.

Mona assesses the stranger's appearance and labels him retro hillbilly hipster. She does this automatically after years of watching a steady parade of Atlanta downtown's oddest and those who wish they were odd come in to Krispy Kreme for a fast hot sugar fix.

I am sure he wasn't born with hair that black, she thinks, continuing to vivisect his appearance. But who can say what color it really is what with all the goop he's got in it. It looks more like an Elvis wig than real hair. He doesn't work out much. Maybe I should deny him a doughnut for health reasons. And he's got a big ass. Can't stand a man with wide hips. Wide hips are for child bearing. And what's with the purple shirt and the rolled up black jeans? Are you supposed to be hillbilly royalty? The only thing that keeps this boy from being total white trash is his boots. Those are some mighty fancy pointy-toed cowboy boots.

"I'm sorry but we close at 12:00 during the week." Mona explains.

"It's only a couple of minutes past midnight. Certainly you wouldn't send me out into the cold night without some hot doughnuts to warm me up?"

With a sigh, Mona starts to point out to the one obstacle keeping her from heading home to the shot of Jack Daniels that awaits her. All the doughnuts have been put to bed along with the machines that make the doughnuts.

But she is speechless. All the display cases are suddenly and miraculously filled with fresh doughnuts of every variety. Behind her she hears the familiar hum of the conveyor belts in action with battalions of cooking donuts marching along.

Mona had always wondered what the saying "blood ran cold" meant. Now she knew.

"How did you do that?"

"How did I do what?"

"Who are you? The devil?"

"Why, yes, I am."

"Are you here for my soul?"

"   No, I'm here for some doughnuts. I'd like one dozen fresh glazed, four chocolate iced with sprinkles, six cinnamon twists, six powdered strawberry filled, six chocolate iced custard filled, six maple glazed, five crullers and six glazed devil's food. Oh yes, and a large cup of regular coffee. None of that decaf crap."

"You've ordered just about everything we got but the glazed lemon filled," Mona said, fumbling for a pen and order pad to write down his request.

"I may be the devil, but even I can't stand those nasty things."

The routine chore of gathering the stranger's order eases Mona's panic and fear. She delivers his order and rings it up. He hands her a fresh one hundred dollar bill. She gives him his change. Instead of leaving, he unloads
his doughnuts and coffee on two of the customer tables and settles his oversized buttocks into a chair with a happy grunt. Mona is not at all surprised that the devil eats with his mouth open.

Business decorum has trapped her. She must wait until he's done before she can leave. But since this is the devil, wouldn't it be permissible to go running out the door, screaming at the top of her lungs? Mona weighs her options and makes a decision. If she is in the clutches of the devil, the real devil himself, then she might as well make the best of a bad situation.

"Tell me something, Mister Devil," she said boldly, "Is Elvis really dead? And if he is, is he in Heaven or Hell?"

The stranger pauses mid-bite.

"I'll be glad to answer any question you have," he said, licking his fingers with loud smacking noises, "But only if you do something for me first."

"You can't take my soul, Evil One!" Mona yells, "I believe in the loving power of Jesus and though I walk in the shadow of the valley of death, I do not fear you."

"Whoa, whoa, whoa! Now don't get your panties in a wad. I don't want your soul. I have plenty, believe me."

"What do you want?" Mona asks suspiciously.

"Show me your tits."

"Show you my what?"

"Your breasts. Your mammaries. Your ta-tas. Pretend it's Mardi Gras and I am on a float about to shower you with cheap strands of beads."

"I don't know. Somehow I get the feeling nothing is that easy with you."

"Suit yourself," he said, resuming his feast.

"I can't believe all the devil wants is to look at my boobs," Mona said. "You are up to something evil. Otherwise, you wouldn't be the devil."

"Mona, let me explain the difference between good and evil," he said lazily. "There's the man who can come in here and order two doughnuts and be satisfied. Then there's the man who comes in and wants all the doughnuts. The problem is inside the man. Don't blame the doughnuts."

Mona crosses her arms tightly over her breasts and thinks about how many doughnuts she could eat in one sitting. Not too many, since she works with them every day. Frankly, doughnuts make her nauseous.

"What would you do if Jesus came walking through that door?" she asks, not expecting an honest answer. "If you really are the devil, then he'd be the last person you'd want to see."

The stranger takes a big gulp of hot coffee and wipes his hand across his mouth, smearing bits of sugar glaze and chocolate over his cheek.

"You know the deal, Mona," he said, "Show me your breasts and I tell you anything you want to know."

"Oh the hell with you," Mona said angrily, "How am I supposed to know you're really the devil? You got no hooves, no horns, no tail. I don't detect the aroma of brimstone on you. Sure you know my name, but it says it right here on my nametag. Sure you got inside a locked door, but anybody with a little criminal know-how could do that. If you really and truly are the devil, then I am not impressed."

The stranger smiled and Mona saw a gleam in his eyes that frightened her.

"Mona Fortune," he said, "Forty-eight years old. Twice divorced, no children. Has worked at this Krisy Kreme for the last ten years. Your favorite drink is Jack Daniels and Mountain Dew, though you like a straight shot of Jack before you go to bed. You drink too much and you smoke too much. You eat too

many fried foods. Everyone you have truly loved is dead. You used to get by on your looks but time, gravity, and abuse are starting to take its toll. You were hoping you could trap
someone with what sex appeal you have left to keep you safe and warm in your old age, but you are beginning to give up on that dream and are thinking of getting more than one cat. How am I doing so far?"

Mona shakes with rage. "Who have you been talking to? Did my ex put you up to this? What kind of sick joke is this?"

"Donny? No Donny didn't put me up to this," said the stranger, "And neither did Billy Jenkins."

"Billy Jenkins," whispers Mona, tears filling her eyes. "How do you know about Billy Jenkins?"

"Show me your breasts and I will tell you all about Billy Jenkins."

"How do you know about Billy Jenkins?" Mona repeats.

"Your breasts have always been your most outstanding feature and they have withstood time well," said the stranger wearily, "But they are on the verge of sagging something terrible. And since neither of us is getting any younger, I will tell you something about Billy Jenkins if it will get me closer to you showing me your breasts. And by the way, can I get a refill on my coffee?"

Mona pours hot coffee into the stranger's outstretched cup. The stranger settles back into his chair and gazes over his boxes, deciding which doughnut to attack next. He chooses a chocolate iced with sprinkles.

"Billy Jenkins," he said between quick bites, "was a boy you dated in high school. You broke the hearts of a lot of boys in high school, but Billy fell really hard for you. He was real country, like you were, and he smelled of earth. He was rough around the edges and though you teased him about his uncouth ways, it made you wet for him. He had big hands and no idea what to do with them. You had every intention of showing him, but there were other boys calling for your attention. Billy would have to wait. But then Billy died in a car accident. He'd been drinking. The day before he died you had teased him for being jealous of your other boyfriends. You blamed yourself for his death. From then on, you used your body as a weapon to punish yourself and any man who dared love you as much as Billy had."

The stranger pulls a wad of napkins out of the dispenser and hands them to Mona. She wipes away her tears and blows her nose.

"Now, Mona, are you ready to show me your tits?"

Mona shivers and looks into the stranger's black eyes.

"Not up here where somebody can see," she said, "Let's go in the back."

The stranger follows Mona to the employee break room. Mona locks the door and then turns to face the stranger. She hesitates, struggling with herself. She pulls her shirt up to her collarbone and then wrestles her bra over her breasts.

The stranger's eyes widen and a sensuous smile spreads across his face. He makes no move towards them. He stares and nods his head for what seems to Mona to be an eternity.

"Are we done now?" she asks irritably.

"Yes, I'm satisfied," answers the stranger. "They are very nice, though I hope you don't mind my saying that I have seen better."

Mona pulls her bra back over her breasts and yanks her shirt back over herself. Her shoulders sag in defeat.

"I could do without the smart-ass comments," she growls, "Now you promised to answer my questions."

"Okay, Mona," he said soothingly, "Elvis and Jesus are both dead, though people's memory of them make them stronger today than when they were alive. Somewhere in the world there are good people being born will do greater things that they did. There are also bad people being born out there who will make Hitler and Charles Manson look like school children. There is nobody in hell who doesn't deserve to be there.

That means Elvis is not in hell, but Colonel Tom is. Billy Jenkins had a drinking problem long before he met you. He inherited it from his father, who whipped him every Friday night. And if you had married Billy, he would have drank and whipped you every Friday night."

"Why did you tell me all this?" asks Mona, "Telling me about Billy, it's almost like you're trying to save me."

"Save you?" said the stranger, looking hurt, "No, my dear Mona, I would never do that. If you continue on the road to ruin, I want it to be because you chose it freely. To do it because you feel some kind of moral obligation to a redneck alcoholic seems damned silly. I already have too many souls in hell for just that reason."

"Well, what happens now?" asks Mona.

The stranger smiles, showing his gleaming white pointed teeth.

"Now you fix me up a fresh box of glazed doughnuts and I'll be on my way."

After the stranger leaves with his box of doughnuts, Mona locks the door behind him and checks it to make sure it's secure. She looks for the stranger, but he's gone. Instead, she stares at the empty road. It has never seemed so cold or dark before.

NCR RADIO TRANSCRIPT

ANNOUNCER: A blessed morning to you all. It's 7:30AM and you're listening to NCR, National Christian Radio. Now the news.

In entertainment news, popular Christian actress Bobbie Sue Sunshine has refused to play a non-believer in the hit TV series "Jesus Loves Me, Don'tcha Know." She said her faith in Jesus is too strong for her to portray a non-believer, even though the producers of the show promised to have her character accept Jesus as her Lord and Savior by mid-season.

In sports, the New England Blessed have accused the San Francisco Crusaders of praying to help them win last week's game after the game had started. This is in violation of league rules, which states that the two teams may only ask for our Savior's guidance before the opening kickoff when both teams pray in unison so as to avoid either team gaining an unfair advantage.

In world news, U.S. armed forces have toppled the Muslim government in Indonesia. Despite violent opposition, the population is being baptized in the glory of Christ. A Pentagon spokesman is reported as saying that the people of Indonesia will understand that they were lost but now are found once they let the love of Christ take over their lives and the U.S. government has had a chance to indoctrinate them. Praise the Lord, Thank you, Jesus.

In politics, the Presidential race has heated up. Senator Jimmy Robertson accused his opponent, Senator Ernest Graham, of having once read a book written by a non-believer that wasn't about the glory of Christ. Senator Graham claims that he was handed the book as he was leaving church years ago and his picture was taken before he even had a chance to look at the cover. He said once he discovered what the book was about, he did not open it, and had an aide burn it immediately.

Former Congressman Chip Randall has died at the age of sixty-four. Randall was the one of the authors of the CHRIST Act. Randall rose to national prominence when he said these words while introducing the CHRIST Act on the floor of the House of Representatives.

CONGRESSMAN RANDALL: Mr. President, tear down this wall between church and state.

ANNOUNCER: As of yet, there has been no official White House statement about Former Congressman Randall's passing.

Coming up next, The Pauly Pilgrim Show. His guest today is Federal Deacon Freeman Wingard. But first, these messages.

COMMERCIAL VOICE TALENT: It's the question no one wants to ask.

Is there a loved one in your family who has lost their way? Do they challenge Jesus' plan for this great country of ours? Have they openly spoken out against the wisdom of our anointed leaders to guide us to the greater glory?

All is not lost.

The Savior Camps are not just for non-Christians and those afflicted with the disease of homosexuality.

Is your faith in God strong enough to report a morally lost family member to your local deputized clergyman or any official affiliate of the National Church? A short stay at a Savior Camp may be just what that loved one needs to regain the ecstasy of Christ in their heart. As the good book says, "Submit yourselves therefore to God. Resist the devil, and he will flee from you. James 4:7."

So, turn in that backslider. Someday he'll thank you.

ANNOUNCER: And now the show hosted by the man some have called the fourteenth apostle- Pauly Pilgrim.

PAULY PILGRIM: A blessed good morning and welcome to the Pauly Pilgrim Show. I'm your host Pauly Pilgrim. My guest today is a true man of God, Federal Deacon Freeman Wingard. He oversees the

Department of Hedge Protection, which keeps our nation secure from the many threats we face both physically and spiritually. Thanks for taking time out of your busy schedule to join us Deacon.

DEACON WINGARD: I'm blessed to be here Pauly.

PILGRIM: The CHIRST Act, an acronym for Christian Households Rising in Support of Truth, declared Christianity as the official religion of the United States of America. Can you believe it's already been ten years since it passed?

WINGARD: It's amazing how far we've come in the last decade, but the CHRIST Act was only a symbolic gesture. Passing the Twenty-eight Amendment, which repealed part of the First Amendment and made it possible for Congress to establish the National Church of Christ is, in my opinion, the official beginning of The Greatest Awakening.

PILGRIM: It really has been amazing to see how the country blossomed once the American people had a chance to see how allowing the Lord Jesus to be the Commander-in-Chief can improve our lives.

WINGARD: As we often said, once you put Jesus in the White House, then all other problems will be solved. Finally, the Christian agenda has taken solid root and the fruits of our labor are ripening across what is simply the greatest, most righteous country in the world.

PILGRIM: There's so much evidence that proves the CHRIST Act led us to becoming a blessed nation. For example, abortion is once again illegal and all forms of birth control are outlawed. Think of all the innocent lives we saved.

WINGARD: Yes brother, can I get an amen?

PILGRIM: Amen, brother.

WINGARD: It wasn't easy. There were many who opposed us. I expected people of lesser religions to object, but I was surprised by the number of people claiming to be Christians who marched in protest.

PILGRIM: You mean the CINOS? Christians in Name Only?

WINGARD: How can you claim to be a true patriot and to love this country and speak out against the will of our Savior? However, that does bring up a painful subject, which is related to today's anniversary. I'm talking about former congressman Chip Randall. He was so instrumental in making this a Christian nation, but sadly, there are times when even prophets lose their way.

PILGRIM: For many years, you worked closely with Chip back before when you were a congressman. How and when did he go astray?

WINGARD: Well Pauly, these things never happen overnight. I should have seen it coming. Chip complained that we were stretching our armed forces too thinly when President Reed designated troops as military missionaries and sent them into countries with unstable governments and ungodly ways. But God's work is never easy and the brave Christian soldiers that we sent into Satan's playgrounds have done a magnificent job.

PILGRIM: Did Chip object to the United States dropping out of the United Nations rather than listen to any more of their stupid resolutions and condemnations?

WINGARD: Oh goodness no. Chip felt we should have left the U.N. years ago. I believe Chip's problem was that he never really understood that God wants us to spread the word of Jesus Christ to the whole world.

PILGRIM: I find that hard to believe.

WINGARD: Let me clarify that statement. Chip understood the need to spread the gospel. He understood that we do this out of love. But I think he was still in the old mindset that our only tools to accomplish this sacred goal were by bearing witness and living a God-fearing life.

PILGRIM: Didn't he understand that sometimes we have to use force to spread God's love?

WINGARD: He really didn't get it. History has taught us that sometimes Christians have to use the sword to save the wicked. Just look at the Crusades. But not only was Chip disturbed about the United States conquering Iraq, Iran, Turkey, Afghanistan, and now Indonesia, it was when the Christian Citizenship law went into effect that he became vocal in his opposition to our holy mission.

PILGRIM: I'm having trouble wrapping my head around that one. The Christian Citizenship Law made it official that only Christians are recognized as citizens. It makes perfect sense. If you're not Christian, you have a choice. Leave or become a Christian.

WINGARD: Exactly. But I believe that's when Chip's faith began to waver. He said to me that he didn't feel it was right for America to force its beliefs on others either here or abroad. He told me to remember that the Pilgrims came to these shores for religious freedom.

PILGRIM: Did you tell him to remember that the Pilgrims came here to be free to worship Jesus Christ as they saw fit? They came here for Christian freedom. I don't think the Pilgrims came here to insure that Muslims and Satanists could do as they please.

WINGARD: It was around this time that Chip Randall and others like him formed the short-lived True Christian Party. I actually agreed with the part of their platform that proclaimed that a true Christian is someone who helps the poor, lives by example, and turns the other cheek. However, when they compared the Savior Camps to Nazi Concentration Camps, I couldn't in good conscious do anything but condemn them publicly as heretics.

PILGRIM: You had no choice, Deacon. Only non-believers who refuse to convert or leave the country are taken to the camps so that their souls can be saved. Sure we round them up and put them in train cars, but only because it's the most economical way to transport large groups of people. Remember, the Nazis herded the Jews into cattle cars and didn't give them food or water. We put them on Amtrak and provide each person with a box lunch and a bottle of water. Sure some liberal elitists complain that all of the box lunches contain ham sandwiches, which neither Jews and Muslims are allowed to eat, but when they get hungry enough, I'm sure they'll eat anything they're given and are thankful for the mercy of Christ upon them.

WINGARD: They usually don't understand until they accept Christ. You have to remember that unlike Christianity, their religions aren't based on love and peace. As I watched Chip being taken away on the train to Montana's Camp Glorious Rebirth, I felt sure that the next time I

saw him, he would have seen the light and we would rejoice in his rebirth. I never would have guessed that he had slipped so far from Christ's path that he would hang himself from the rafters of his bunkhouse.

PILGRIM: Hold on, Deacon. Maybe we should change the subject. There's been no official statement as to how Chip Randall died.

WINGARD: As deacon of Hedge Protection, I felt it was my duty to go Camp Glorious Rebirth and see for myself. Chip had twisted his bed sheet into a noose and hung himself on a rafter. In his own blood, he wrote on the rafter, "If we say we have no sin, we deceive ourselves, and the truth is not in us. John 1:8." Who do you think he wrote those words for?

PILGRIM: I'm not sure we should be discussing this, but I can't help but point out that by committing suicide, Chip Randall will never be allowed into heaven.

WINGARD: True. But I can't help thinking that maybe when he wrote that bible verse; he was trying to tell us something. Could we be deceiving ourselves into believing that we have no sin? By trying to save America, have we instead destroyed our great nation?

PILGRIM: If I didn't know better I'd say it sounds like your faith in the righteousness of our proud Christian nation is wavering. Tell me Deacon, do you feel the need to take a short vacation at a savior camp?

WINGARD: Of course not! Do you?

PILGRIM: (laughs) Hey, I was just joking.

WINGARD: Well, whatever message Chip Randall was trying to leave us, it will remain a mystery forever. The camp staff cleaned and painted the rafter. It's as if it never happened.

PILGRIM: Well, Deacon, I can see my producer waving at me, which means we have to take a commercial break. When we come back, Deacon Wingard and I will discuss the government's latest predictions of when we can expect the Second Coming. Don't go away, your weekend plans may depend on this report.

COMMERCIAL VOICE TALENT: Don't miss Mega-Mart's End of Days Sale. With our nation in the hands of our Lord, it's only a matter of time before the rapture comes! Enjoy the material things of life before Jesus takes us all to heaven.

This week's special is stereo systems. We have speakers with fidclity so clear, we'd swear that you could hear the angels through them, that is if we swore, which we don't because taking the Lord's name in vain is a sin and a crime that will get you put in jail.

Worried about overextending your credit card or going in debt? Just remember, there are no overdue bills in heaven. So hurry on down to your local Mega-Mart for the End of Days Sale. Hurry up or everything will be gone before you're gone from this earth.

THE CARPORT

"Let's not go inside just yet," Sharon said, placing her hand on Dave's lap.

Sharon leaned over and kissed Dave. It was a lingering kiss with her breast pressed against his arm. Dave felt an erection growing. Sharon's hand slipping between his legs and gently squeezing his crotch helped too. After the kiss, Sharon sat back in her seat and smiled her best sexy smile.

They had just returned home from a rare dinner date. All of Dave's friends with children had teased him that once Hannah arrived there would be no more going out until she was old enough to go on dates herself and by then, Dave would be too old and tired to go out. Dave knew they were kidding, even if there was a kernel of truth to what they said. Despite the exhaustion of caring for a newborn, Dave and Sharon hadn't wanted to spend a minute away from their precious infant daughter.

When Sharon's mother, Delores, came to visit, she insisted that Dave and Sharon go out and leave her to babysit.

"Don't worry," Delores said. "I have some experience in this area. You two need a break, even if you don't realize you need one."

Dave and Sharon finally relented and made a reservation at their favorite Italian restaurant. During dinner, Dave found himself staring at Sharon and remembering how much she turned him on. She had dressed up in a tight blue dress and fishnet stocking.

"I'm tempted to take you to a hotel room after dinner," Dave said.

"I'm tempted to let you," Sharon said.

But they didn't go to a hotel. They wanted to get home to their daughter and they didn't want to waste the money on a hotel room. After dinner, they drove straight home. Dave figured the night was over, but then Sharon had put her hand in his lap.

"You want to do something here?" Dave asked. "In the car?"

"I don't really feel like climbing into the back seat," Sharon said. She reached over and unbuckled Dave's belt. "I just want to play around. Maybe this could be all about you."

Dave was no longer starting to get hard. He was hard. Really hard. He slouched down in the driver's seat so Sharon would have easier access to his pants. The car was parked in the carport, which sat on the edge of their small back yard. Dave looked at the house to see if any of the lights were on. The house was dark.

"What about Delores?" Dave asked.

"She never stays up past nine," Sharon said. "And Hannah has been sleeping through the night lately. They're both asleep."

Sharon pulled down the zipper to Dave's pants and yanked them open. She traced the outline of his straining penis with her forefinger on the outside of his underwear. Dave closed his eyes and sucked in air between his teeth.

"As long as you're sure," Dave said.

"Stop worrying," Sharon said.

Sharon worked her hand under the elastic band of Dave's underwear. When her hand found his penis, she gripped the shaft and leaned over and kissed Dave's neck.

Dave wanted to give in to the pleasure of Sharon's expert hands and mouth and whatever else she decided to use to blow his mind, but the back yard was so small, which made the house so close. The house where his mother-in-law was inside right now, sleeping and hopefully not peeking out the window and wondering why he and Sharon hadn't gotten out of the car already.

"We couldn't make love in the house tonight, could we?" Dave said, "Not with your mom in the next room."

"No," Sharon said, "That would be gross."

Sharon pulled down Dave's underwear. His penis, freed from its tight cotton confinement, stood straight up in the open air. Sharon ran her fingernails gently up and down the side. Dave's toes curled.

"But isn't the carport like part of the house?" Dave said.

Sharon's open mouth was an inch away from the tip of Dave's penis when she stopped.

"No, the carport is not part of the house," she said, "The carport is outside of the house."

"Isn't that just a technicality?" Dave said. "The carport is still part of the property. When we say this is our home, we mean the house, the yard, and the carport. I can show you on the property map."

"Yes, it's all our property," Sharon said, "but mom is inside the house sleeping and we are outside in our car, where nobody can see us. Now, do you want a blowjob or not?"

"I love your blowjobs," Dave said, "but I can't stop thinking about how your mother is like right there."

Dave pointed at the house.

"You're starting to make me think about my mother," Sharon said, "and I find that very disturbing. Would you rather we didn't do this?"

Dave looked down at his erect penis. Then he looked at Sharon. She was so beautiful and the dress really showed off her breasts. Dave put his hand on Sharon's thigh and sighed.

"What to do, what to do," he said.

"I think it's time for you to let the little head do the thinking for the big head," Sharon said, "because right now, the big head is thinking about all this way too much."

"Convince me," Dave said.

Dave got to see Sharon's sexy smile again before she bent over and wrapped her lips around his penis. He leaned back and closed his eyes. Her mouth kept going down until her nose rubbed against his pubic hair.

Through half-opened eyes, Dave looked down at Sharon's bobbing head. He wondered where she learned to do that thing with her tongue? He wondered how he got to be such a lucky bastard to be with a woman who loved to give head? He wondered if he didn't see a light come on in the house? Was someone looking out of the guest room window?

Forget it about it, Dave thought. He closed his eyes and decided that Sharon was right. Sometimes you had to let the little head do the thinking for the big head.

THE GIRL IN THE LUMPY SWEATER

I get a lot of crap from the guys at work for dating Sandra. Like I give a damn what they think. All they see is her lumpy, shapeless sweaters and her wide floor length skirts. The poor blind bastards! They'll never be lucky enough to see her as I'm seeing right now in my bedroom.

As soon as she showed up at my apartment door tonight, I started my carnal advances. Rather than give her a simple hello kiss, I held her face in my hands and kissed her passionately, shoving my tongue deep into her mouth. Our tongues played hide and seek with each other while our bodies shifted closer together. We unlocked our lips and I worked my way down her neck, nipping gently on the supple flesh. I scooped my hands around her ass and squeezed it hard, but not too hard. Sandra giggled and dug her fingers into my shoulders. She leaned into my chest and bit my lower lip. The heat of passion was rising quickly between us. At least, I know I was rising quickly. Whatever plans we had for the evening would just have to wait. My dick was straining painfully to be freed from the confines of my pants. I was going to need some sexual satisfaction soon or else. It was obvious that Sandra felt the same way when she took my hand and led me into the bedroom.

Which brings me to where I am now, watching her unzip her long skirt and let it fall to the floor. I follow her lead by unbuckling my belt and pulling off my pants. I pause from undressing any further so that I can watch as her pulls off her sweater. For the briefest moment I remember the jeers of the guys at work, ridiculing me for dating big lumpy Sandra. What they don't know is that underneath her formless attire, she's hiding a deliciously curvaceous body topped with the largest bra-bursting jugs I've ever seen. Every time I see them, it takes my breath away. This time is no exception.

Her hand starts to pull down her bra strap then stops. I resist the urge to reach over and yank it down myself. She always hesitates at this moment. Taking a deep breath, she pulls the bra strap the rest of the way. Her massive tit pops out of the confining cup. Quickly, she pulls the other strap down and soon the bra is discarded completely. I study every detail of her wonderfully large, soft breasts. I step over to her and cup my hands under her massive mounds, feeling their impressive weight. I'm constantly amazed at how they stand up on their own, considering their incredible size.

"44 DD," she said, guessing the question in my mind, "Have you ever seen anything so grotesque in your entire life?"

Suddenly, she pulls away from me and throws herself down on the bed. She buries her face in the pillow and begins to sob. I kneel down next to her and wrap my arms around her waist. My searching fingers try to find her pert nipples. She stymies my efforts by rolling away and hugging her arms around her chest. I'm burning with the desire to bury my throbbing erection between her glorious golden gazoongas. But first, I have to convince her that deep down she wants me to titfuck her. I believe that if I do this right, she'll beg me to cream all over her tits.

"Come on, Sandra," I said gently, holding her tight, "Don't cry. You're so beautiful and you just can't see it. Here, let me prove to you how beautiful you are."

I take her hand and guide it to my erection. Her fingers curl around it and squeeze. She sits up and faces me, her hand still clutching my cock tightly.

"Oh, Jeff," she sighs, her face streaked with tears, "You are so good to me."

Then she yanks my underwear off, allowing my dick to expand to its full length. She pushes me back on the bed, and then positions her head over my groin. She hesitates for a moment to admire the impressive size of my prick and then her open mouth swallows it almost to the base. Oh man, that tongue of hers is velvet smooth. She bobs her head up and down, making delightful sucking noises. I lay my head back on the pillow and soak in the waves of sensations her mouth is giving me. Her warm tongue flickers up my shaft and then circles the knob. Shivers of electricity shoot up spine. Despite being in blowjob heaven, my mind still keeps trying to comprehend why this gorgeous woman believes so staunchly that she is an ugly freak. Standing at 5' 6", 140 lbs. with long auburn hair, lush lashes over hazel eyes, full generous lips just below her cute upturned nose, sturdy legs that end on the nicest curved ass I've ever seen, and not an inch of her surgically enhanced; she is the perfect woman. So why is she convinced that she's anything but the most fuckable babe on this planet? She thinks her tits are too big! Can you believe it? There is no such thing as too big when it comes to tits! Her tongue running along the base of my balls brings my attention back to where it belongs. I push my concerns about her false self-image out of my mind for the moment and concentrate on the here and now. I grab her head and start fucking her mouth. She reaches her hands around and gets a firm grip on my ass cheeks. Her silky hair rubbing against my stomach adds to my mounting excitement. I consider holding back, but that only lasts a second before I start shooting my creamy load down her throat. She gobbles it hungrily and then licks me clean. I pull her up to me and begin kissing the slope of her neck. I maneuver down to lick her nipple but she pulls her breast away, which isn't easy with tits as large as hers. She pulls the bed sheet as best she can over her oversized chest. Her fingers clutch the fabric tight against her chin. I can tell that I'm not going to get any nearer her tits tonight. I imagine choking the neck of the person that convinced her to be ashamed of her stupendous breasts. And I know where the bitch lives too. Unfortunately, the bitch is Sandra's mother.

Sandra's mother is a very religious woman. There's nothing wrong with that, but she's also a very bitter woman. Sex, in her mind, is repulsive and wicked and should be avoided. Her attitude made no sense to me until I found out that her husband, Sandra's father, left her for a woman with big tits. From that day on, she turned away from sex. The Bible became her only comfort from the pain she carried inside.

To make matters worse, Sandra developed humongous hooters, just like the woman her dad left her mother for. Sandra must have gotten her overgrown mammaries from her dad's side of the family, because her mom sure as hell wasn't lucky in that department. The larger Sandra's breast grew, the more her mother drilled it into her head to be ashamed of her boobs and repulsed by her body's natural sexuality. And since this is a very small town, it was easy for her mother to keep a tight rein on Sandra's life.

Being with me is the first time in her twenty-four years that Sandra has ever tried to move away from her mother's twisted influence.

Before I met Sandra, I thought getting transferred to this backwater town was the worst thing that ever happened to me. My company made out like a bandit setting up a district office here. First, they got all kinds of government incentives. Then, since the country's booming economy had somehow passed over this sleepy little hamlet, the local community was more than willing to work for substandard pay. I almost turned down the assignment, but my company gave me all kinds of incentives. They offered me an executive position and when it came to my salary, let's just say they held a loaded checkbook to my head. I couldn't say no. However, once I got here I learned that my generous salary meant nothing since there didn't seem anything here to spend it on. I was pretty

depressed about the whole deal until Sandra came along.

I almost didn't meet her. She's a clerk in our accounting department and I just happen to stop in their office to clear up a mistake they made on my 401K. I was pretty steamed at the time, but then I saw Sandra bending over a file cabinet and completely forgot why I had come in there. She was wearing one of her trademark big heavy sweaters and baggy slacks, which gave the impression she was really fat. But even dressed as she was, I knew better. Her oversized sweater couldn't disguise the two round impressions her oversized breasts made against the material. Soon I was making any excuse I could to stop in and chat with her. I couldn't tell whether she appreciated my initial advances or not. Her shyness and insecurity kept me at arm's length. I wracked my brain for a plan to make the connection without resorting to blatant sexual harassment.

All of my plans went out the window during one of our company functions. I foolishly had way too much to drink. The alcohol drowned my common sense and my lust took over. I stumbled up to her and blurted out, "Sandra, I want to fuck you." As soon as I said the words, I was sure that I had totally screwed up. I imagined myself trying to explain my actions to my superiors before the authorities hauled me off to jail. To my amazement she said, "Okay." Later she told me that she was so taken back that somebody desired her, she didn't dare say no. Also, she'd been waiting for a chance to rebel against her mother and having sex with me was the perfect place to start. We left the party that night without another word between us and went directly to my place.

We've been screwing regularly ever since. Despite her initial inexperience in the bedroom, she's become quite adept at keeping me happy. Well, almost. Twenty-four is a long time to wait to start having sex and she's been very eager to catch up. She's always willing to go along with anything I suggest doing, except when it comes to her tits. She barely even lets me see them. She usually turns out the lights or gets under the covers before taking off her bra. Sometimes she even tries to keep it on. The number her mother did on her head just goes too deep. As much as she craves and enjoys having sex with me, she can't stop thinking of her body as being repulsive. The whole situation is driving me nuts.

If I weren't such a dedicated tit man and if hers weren't so damn perfect, maybe it wouldn't bother me so much. I know instinctively that if I push her too hard, she'll run away for good. If we can't get around this problem, then I'll have to stop seeing her.

I've tried every way I can think of to show her how sexy mammoth tits can be. As a dedicated tit man, I've accumulated an impressive collection of big boob magazines and videos. She looks just as good and sometimes better than many of the outstanding babes featured in my collection. But when I tried to show them to her, her mother's distorted teachings got in the way. She felt it was too shameful to even glance at them!

At this moment, after another unsuccessful attempt to get my hands on her luscious mounds of soft tit flesh, I turn to my collection for solace.

134

She's pretending to be asleep, so I put on my robe and go into the living room. I select one of my favorite videos and insert it into the VCR. On the TV screen flickers an image of a beautiful blond with overripe breasts giving some lucky bastard the blowjob of his life. After getting his tool wet and slippery with her saliva, she mashes it between her tits. I flop down on the couch and enjoy the show. The camera lingers on a tight close-up of his rigid tool pumping between her heavenly milkbags. I start to feel myself get hard. There's a melancholy ache in my balls from the knowledge that I have the real thing in the next room and can't to do a damn thing about it.

Suddenly, I hear a voice behind me say, "She's so beautiful!"

I turn around and there's Sandra standing behind me, wearing my bed sheet like a sarong. Her eyes are riveted to the screen.

"Yeah, she looks mighty fine," I reply, "But I've seen better."

"Really?" she asks, "Where?"

"Look in the mirror."

Slowly, as if in a trance, she walks back into the bedroom and turns on the light. She stands in front of the full-length mirror on the wall. She unwraps the sheet and lets it fall to the floor. She stares at her naked body as if she's seeing it for the first time. She arches her back and thrusts out her breasts. Her hands reach up and gingerly finger her nipples. Her face turns red, first from shame, then from desire.

She comes back to the living room. The light from the TV outlines her body, giving her a sensuous glow. I stand up and place my palms tentatively on her breasts. She lets out a tiny gasp, and then nods her head. I bend down and suck her distended nipple until it's hard as a
bullet. Then I move to the other one and do the same. Sandra runs her fingers through my hair and hugs my face into her expansive cleavage.

"Sit down," she whispers into my ear.

I obey her command and sit down on the couch. She reaches down and opens my robe. My dick is standing straight up and is hard enough to slice granite. She pushes my legs apart, and then kneels between them. With one of her hands, she guides my engorged cock between her glorious orbs. Once in position, she shifts both her hands to the outside of her breasts and pushes them together, squeezing it inside. She licks the tip of the head where it's sticking out of the top of her pressed cleavage. She gets it good and wet. My hands are clutching the couch cushions on either side of me because the feeling is driving me insane

I don't know what made her stop hating her tits. I'd like to think I finally convinced her that they're beautiful and sexy. I don't dare stop her from what she's doing to ask her.

My head is spinning from having my cock immersed in warm, spongy flesh. Slowly at first, then quicker and quicker she moves her mammoth breasts up and down. Again and again, my rigid prod disappears between her tits. Each time the head pops her waiting tongue gives it a generous lick. At first, I can't tear my eyes off what is happening to me. But then, I look at her face and see how she's also getting off on it. Her eyes are little slits and her breathing is heavy. I reach down and massage her pink stiff nipples. This gets her off even more. Her flushed cheeks indicate to me that she's working herself up to an orgasm. Her breasts must be so sensitive that she can come from tit fucking alone. But I'm not ready to deliver her first pearl necklace yet. I grab her shoulders and pull her up. She's dazed and confused by my actions. She was so close and can't believe I'm stopping her.

Before she can protest, I turn her around and bend her over on the couch. I guide my dick to her dripping wet pussy. For the first time, I notice the strong lusty scent pouring out of her glistening orifice. I slam into her fast enough to make her gasp out loud. She's burning hot inside as her cunt muscles clamp down tight around my dick. I pump in and out of her as hard as I can. The sound of my balls slapping against her ass makes us both crazy. I've never heard her moan this much and soon those moans turn to shouts. The shouts are raw, guttural animal sounds. Her ass is quivering from her impending orgasm. I grab her pelvis to keep her steady. I love getting a good hold on a woman's ass when I fuck her from behind so that she knows that I have total control over her. That way she can really let loose. And that's exactly what Sandra does when her orgasm rips through her. She lets out one long ear-splitting scream of ecstasy. Her cunt muscles vibrate wildly over my dick. Her come dribbles over my dick, out of her vagina and down my balls.

I slide out of her soaking pussy. She rolls over on her back, her breathing heavy from all the exertion. I ease myself down next to her. My dick is still rock hard. A film of shiny sweat covers her body and her eyes are heavy with sated lust. I smile at her, knowing I've finally gotten through to her. The sexy woman I knew was inside her is fully released. But there's one more test and it has to be her choice. She knows it too. Without saying a word, she kneels back down between my knees and puts my dick back between her breasts. It's drenched in her come so it has more lubrication than it needs.

"This time," she coos, "Don't deny me. I beg you. Please cover me with your come. I want ever drop on my big, bouncy, beautiful boobies."

Again, she places her hands on either side of her tits, making a nice tight but still slippery nest for my dick. Again, she starts to manipulate her mashed breasts up and down. I brace my legs and reach down with my hands to tweak her now red hot nipples. I feel a shiver run from her body all the way to the base of my ass.

After just a few strokes, she whimpers, "I'm going to come again. Will you come too?"

How can I turn down a request like that? My swollen rod jerks violently as gobs of gooey sperm squirts out onto her oversized melons. She squeezes those melons even tighter as another orgasm ripples through her body.

Once the waves of our mutual climax subside, we collapse together, completely spent and sated. After a while, she sits up and admires the sperm dripping off her boobs. She lifts one of them and licked a big glob into her mouth.

"Never has your come tasted so sweet," she said with the biggest grin I've ever seen on her glowing face.

Since that night, Sandra has developed a whole new attitude about her body. She wears tight, low cut blouses and short shirts. She wears dangerously high heels so that her ass really sticks out. When she walks, she swings her hips. In the office, guys' jaws drop and run into office furniture whenever she goes by. Then they glare at me with jealous rage. Finally the stupid bastards see what I've always known about her. And they're too late to do anything about it. The "lumpy" girl is all mine. The women in the office save their jealous stares for Sandra. We just smile back and say nothing. Screw 'em.

In the bedroom, her sexual appetite is unbridled. She's constantly coming up with something new to try out. One of her latest was that we buy a video camera so that we can act out some of our favorite scenes from my video collection. Part of me is tempted to send a copy of one of our homemade tapes to her mother. Let her see that the sick mind fuck she did on her daughter has finally been broken. But it's not necessary. All anyone has to do is look at Sandra today to see how proud she is of her gorgeous gigantic breasts.

THE BRA MAN COMETH

"Are you the Bra Man?" I asked.

I knew he wasn't, but he was the only person in the narrow shop dominated by floor to ceiling shelves, overstuffed with countless thin rectangular boxes. He was too young and far too cute to be the Bra Man.

The article I'd read about this discount lingerie shop included a photo of the legendary Bra Man, a middle-aged, overweight Orthodox Jew who had the uncanny ability to look at any woman and immediately tell what size bra she wore. He shouted it out like a carnival barker guessing your weight only he was always right.

You would think nobody would be better at determining what size bra should hold a woman's breasts than the woman herself. But you'd be wrong. We totally suck at picking out what's best for ourselves, which might explain why we end up in so many fucked-up relationships.

Wearing the wrong bra, like dating the wrong man, can lead to years of cut shoulders and misery, especially if you have large breasts like mine. Large isn't a big enough word to describe them. Huge, honking, come to mama, bigger than your head breasts was more like it. The kind men worshipped and girlfriends envied. No frilly thing from Victoria's Secret was going to hold these boulders.

From the way he was staring, I could tell the cute guy liked my impressive rack. I could also tell he was sweet from the way he tore his dark brown eyes away from my tits to look me in the eye when he spoke.

"No," he said, "That's my father. He's gone for the day. You know, its Friday."

Oh fuck, it was Friday afternoon. Every Orthodox Jew in town had already closed up shop for the Sabbath. That meant he also wouldn't be in tomorrow. I was devastated. I had no idea when I'd find the time to come back here for my perfect bra.

"Then what are you doing here?" I asked. He had the dangling sideburns and the beanie of an Orthodox Jew.

"I'm running a little late today, so sue me," he said with a shrug. "Don't tell my father, but I don't take the rules of Sabbath as seriously as he does. For instance, if a customer like yourself needs help, then I'm willing to stay past sundown to attend to her needs."

This was an interesting twist. I've always been impressed with how seriously his people took the Sabbath, refusing to do even simple things like turn on a light from sundown on Friday to sundown on Saturday. He was the first one I'd met who was willing to bend the rules.

"Is there something I could help you with?" he asked with a sly smile.

I saw where he was going. It was the end of the workday. We were alone. There was little chance of another customer coming in.

I was tempted. He was seriously cute and his appreciative ogling of my tits had already gotten my nipples erect. My nipples weren't the only thing erect. I could see the bulge in his pants from his certainly circumcised cock.

But I really needed a bra. The boy was going to have to work for his reward.

"Do you have the same gift as your father?" I demanded.

"For determining a woman's bra size? My methods are different, but yes, I can tell you what your correct size is. What size do you wear now?"

"38 Double D."

"No, that's not right. I would guess you're closer to a 40 Triple D."

"What do you mean, you guess? Don't you know for sure?"

He gave me that sly smile again. Had I fallen into a trap?

"Like I said, my method is different from my father's. He can tell by looking," he said, stepping close enough for me to smell his cologne, musky with a hint of tangy citrus. "I can tell by touching."

My heart started racing and I felt an itch between my legs.

"Is there some place we can go that's a little more private?" I asked huskily.

He quickly stepped around me and locked the front door. There was no turning back now. With a nod of his head, he led me to the dressing room. It was located in the back of the store. It wasn't actually a room, just a flowered bed sheet that served as a door and a cheap full-length mirror propped against the wall. There were more shelves with more boxes along the walls. The room was so tiny we had to stand within inches of each other. It had a down and dirty feel to it that increased my excitement.

"Take off your shirt and bra," he instructed.

I slowly unbuttoned my shirt and felt a tingling cool breeze as I slid it off my shoulders. He breathed in deep and held his breath as I pulled my bra straps down one at a time, allowing one of my large firm tits to pop out followed closely by the other. My nipples pointed out hard and ready. He let his breath out with an appreciative sigh.

He reached out and cupped his hands around my tits. His touch was firm as his fingers slid around the full width of my massive flesh. His thumbs teased my nipples for a second before they flitted away.

"I was right," he said, "40 Triple D. Wait right here."

It wasn't until he had spoken that I realized that I had closed my eyes during his breast examination. I had been savoring the sensation of his fingers. When I opened my eyes, I found I was alone. I wanted to go find him. I wanted him to touch me some more. But I desperately needed a new bra, so I waited.

As I stood there, topless, I wondered how many women had been in this cramped space before me with their tits hanging out, waiting for the Bra Man to return. I scanned the walls for a security camera. Nothing would piss me off more than to find photos of my boobs on the Internet, especially if I didn't get paid for it.

There was no sign of a camera, but I found a framed photo of a man and a boy hanging between the shelves. The resemblance between them was obvious; this was a father and son. They're wearing prayer shawls over their black suits. I could only guess from the proud smiles on their faces that they were celebrating the boy's bar mitzvah. The man I recognized as the Bra Man. The boy was a younger version of the man I was waiting for. He had the same curly hair and sly look in his eye.

I felt oddly embarrassed with them smiling down at me. Reflexively I covered my exposed nipples with my hands. I wondered why it was taking him such a long time to find those damn bras. I was thinking that maybe this wasn't such a great idea. I was about to reach for my shirt when he returned.

In his arms was a stack of rectangular boxes. He opened the boxes to reveal 40 Triple D bras in a rainbow of colors. He made a big show of opening one box, which contained a sleek black bra that managed to look sturdy and sexy at the same time.

I tried it on first. It was amazing. It fit perfectly. For the first time in decades my breasts were lifted and separated and comfortable. I tried on another and another, each with the same result. I had found the perfect bras. I thought I was going to faint right there on that filthy floor.

"Now, keep one thing in mind about these bras," he said cautiously.

"They turn into pumpkins at midnight?" I asked.

"No," he said, as he avoided the obvious pumpkin joke, "Remember that these are discount bras."

"Does that mean they're no good?"

"No, they're good bras. In fact, they're great bras and just as good as the ones you buy in the finest department stores. Only these bras cost thirty percent less."

I swear to God I came in my pants right then and there.

"Could I wear one of these home," I asked, "I mean, after I pay for it?"

"Of course," he said, "We aim to please the customer."

"Could I give the salesman a tip for all his hard work?"

"Sure," he said, "I want my customers to be happy."

I pulled him to me and slid my hands down around his small tight ass. His lips met mine and his tongue snaked its way into my mouth. He reached his hand around my back and in one deft motion undid my bra and slipped it off. He really was a bra man. The industrial hooks that come with bras like mine are a fortress of steel. He had taken mine off like he was peeling Velcro.

He brought his hands around and grabbed my tits hungrily. His touch was urgent but never painful. He bent his head down and sucked on my red aching nipples. I thought they would burst; they were swollen so full. His tongue played equal time with each stiffened nipple. I reached down for his crotch. My fingers slid around his trapped erection. He wasn't the only one who could tell someone's size by feel. Eight and a half inches was my educated guess. I unbuckled his belt and savored the sound of his zipper coming down. He took a step back and yanked his pants and tighty whities down to his ankles.

My size prediction was correct!

He undressed completely and made a bed on the floor with his clothes as his erect penis bobbed up and down. I took off the rest of my clothes. We stood for a moment and admired each other's bodies. I kneeled down on the floor in front of him. I watched his face as I took his penis in my hand and licked my lips. He moaned softly and his penis squirmed in my fist. I love that first sensation of putting a hard prick in my mouth. The salty taste of pre-come, the urgent throbbing, the yearning to begin the painful pleasure. When I put a man's dick in my mouth, I own him. I sucked him until I had covered his penis with a good glistening coat of spit. I popped it out of my mouth and placed it between my tits. I pressed them together to make a nice snug cave. His eyes squeezed shut as he tit-fucked me furiously. I wanted him to fuck me in the worst way but the thought of him spewing hot sperm all over my massive breasts had its appeal too. Fuck it! Go with the moment. Whichever way he came I was going to enjoy it. From the way his penis was quivering, it was going to be soon.

He pulled away from me at the last possible moment and kneeled down on the floor next to me.

"Get on top of me," he said in a hoarse whisper, "I want to play with your tits while we fuck."

He lay down on the floor, his dick a flagpole standing at attention. I straddled my firm legs on either side of his slender hips and guided the purple head of his dick to my tender cunt-lips. For a moment I held him there at the entrance of a cave that led to the core of my desire. We both ached with the need to fuck our brains out. In one quick motion, I slid him into me. My pussy gave no resistance. Slick with natural lubrication, it opened freely and easily as I impaled myself on the full length of his rigid cock.

I threw back my shoulders and grabbed his thighs for support. Foreplay was over; I was riding his dick as hard and as fast as I could go. My thoughts blurred as flames burning from my crotch to my ears consumed my body. I felt his hands roaming over me, squeezing the fleshy cheeks of my ass, pinching the erect nipples of my enormous breasts, and gripping my hips so he could grind into me harder and harder and harder.

I could feel an orgasm volcano growing inside me. The kind that when it erupts, it makes your hips

shake, your bowels wink and your tongue hang out the side of your mouth. But it was a slippery thing hiding inside my womb, so I used his stiff pole to hunt it down. I speeded up the rhythm of our fucking so it wouldn't get away. The sound of our sweaty bodies slapping
against each other made me think of a galloping stallion racing for the finish line.

I looked up and noticed the framed photo again. His father's face beamed with pride. What would he have thought if he could have seen his little boy right then?

"When you gave your bar mitzvah speech," I said between ragged breaths, "did you start with the words, 'today, I am a man'?"

A grin spread across his face. "Yes, I think I did."

"Well, today you are THE MAN!" I shouted.

My first orgasm shivered up through me and released so fast, I almost didn't realized I had come until I felt the next three ripping through me. I couldn't stop coming. My cunt juices dribbled down his balls and left a puddle on his clothes beneath us. It was like we were swimming in our combined body fluids. I laughed, a mixture of relief and joy. He grabbed my tits firmly and I grabbed his wrists for support. We didn't want to slide away from each other. We weren't done yet.

I felt something hit my head. It wasn't hard or heavy, just annoying. Then another and another. We were thrashing around so violently that we were knocking the rectangular boxes of bras off their shelves. Black bras with delicate lace, sturdy white sports bras, simple flat training bras, purple and misty green full cup bras and coral bras with hidden supports and a cute red rose stitched between the cups littered the floor around us. All I could think was that I wasn't going to be the one to clean up this mess.

That would be the sexy man below me. I looked down into his eyes just as he was about to come. His face was flushed and his eyes were glazed with sweet agony. His dick wanted release but his body kept holding back until the last possible moment.

Then he exploded inside me. His molten sperm gushed into my cunt, causing me to have one last shaking orgasm. Then I collapsed on top of him, glistening and spent. My body jerked from the tremors of mini orgasms, like little earthquakes.

We lay there in a heap, holding onto each other as our bodies cooled. Slowly and reluctantly, I peeled my sticky body off of his and surveyed the mayhem our fucking has caused. It was a glorious mess. I had a big stupid grin on my face, the one you get after a really good fuck.

I looked down at the man who had given me this sexual satisfaction. He was still sprawled on the ground with his eyes closed, cradling his head in his hands. He seemed mighty proud of himself. He should be. Despite the ache in my ravaged cunt, I felt the urge to start all over. Maybe some other time.

But then I looked at his long curly sideburns and his beautiful circumcised dick. We were from different worlds. He was an orthodox Jew. I wasn't. If he brought me, a non-Jewish girl, home to meet his parents, they'd disown him on the spot.

Damn, I only went in there for a bra. I didn't need to take that kind of shit home with me. I put the whole idea out of my head. It was a great fuck. Leave it at that.

We dressed and he gathered up my bras and put them in a shopping bag.

"So what do I owe you for the bras?" I asked.

"Just your phone number," he said.

"Are you sure about that?" I asked. It hurt knowing that even if I gave him my number, once I was gone, he'd realized he could never call me.

He must have known what I was thinking. He said, "Yes, I really do. I haven't decided if this is for me yet."

He held out his arms like he was referring to the store, but he was talking about so much more.

"I think a woman like you might help me decide where I belong. It's a bit much to ask, I know."

"Don't say anything more," I said as I reached into my purse for a pen and one of my business cards. I wrote my cell phone number down on the back.

He slipped my card carefully into his breast pocket. As I turned to leave, he gently put his hand on mine.

"Would you by any chance be in the mood for… you know," he said with that same sly grin.

I felt that itch between my legs again. Besides, I wasn't in a hurry to get anywhere. This time we made love slower and with more deliberation. He climbed on top of me, and I wrapped my strong legs tightly around his waist. He nibbled my swollen nipples, as I dug my fingers into his soft curly hair. I thought I would be too sore after the ravishing he'd given my pussy earlier, but I was wrong. He prick slid into me like it was coming home. His balls bounced against my ass as he picked up the pace of his thrusts. I was certain there was no way I could have another orgasm. Again, I was wrong.

My orgasm vibrated through me from my ass to my toes, and back up to my tits and my scalp. He came with me, his hot and gooey sperm shooting into my womb.

Afterwards, I stood up and my legs were wobbly. My pubic bone was rubbed raw. It was the kind of ache you get after a really good workout. I had on just my panties and was about to decide which of my new bras to wear when he presented me with a gift. It was a beautiful, full figure red lace bra with the softest shoulder straps I've ever touched and an embroidered heart between the cups. I tried it on. The weight of my breasts was magically gone. It was like someone had wrapped them into a silk hammock and was carrying them for me. After I finished dressing, I gave him a long lingering thank you kiss.

And then I left the store with my new bras, and someone who might just be a perfect fit for me.

NOTHING IN ANYBODY'S ASS

Scene: Bob and Rita are eating brunch at a hip bistro. Their relationship has progressed to the point where they feel comfortable asking each other personal questions.

Bob: How many men have you slept with?

Rita: I honestly don't know. I've lost count. Does that bother you?

Bob: No. Really it doesn't. How many women have you slept with?

Rita: Okay, that number I know. Fifteen.

Bob: So a definite preference for men. Good to know.

Rita: How many women have you slept with?

Bob: Like you, I've lost count.

Rita: How many men?

Bob: Five. But with two of those guys, I was part of a three way with a woman. You know how it is.

Rita: Oh sure. You want to try as many combinations you can.

Bob: Exactly.

Rita: Where do you stand on anal sex?

Bob: I tried it once and didn't like it.

Rita: Really? Most men I hook up with are constantly trying to stick their penis in my ass.

Bob: Oh you mean where I stick *my* penis in somebody's ass. I tried it once and I didn't like it.

Rita: So we agree. Nothing in anybody's ass.

Bob: BDSM?

Rita: Too complicated and I always forget the safe word.

Bob: I'm terrible with knots.

Rita: Roleplay?

Bob: It's okay as long as it's not too elaborate or involves expensive costumes.

Rita: Spanking?

Bob: My hand gets tired really fast.

Rita: Kids?

Bob: You mean having kids? You're not talking about having sex with kids.

Rita: Oh God no! I meant having kids. Not like right now, but eventually.

Bob: I like kids.

Rita: I like you.

Bob: I like you too.

SPIKES

Opal had just taken the bread out of the oven to cool when her phone rang. She took her time walking from the kitchen to the living room of her luxury apartment. The phone on the coffee table vibrated each time it rang. The Caller Id informed her that the call was from her best friend, Nikki.

"What's up, girl," Opal said.

"Where the hell are you?" Nikki said. "I'm here at Dawgie Daddy's and the place is packed with hungry wolves. I can't handle them all myself."

Opal could hear people shouting to be heard over the blaring dance music. She could picture the scene at Dawgie Daddy's. Men dressed in their one good suit wearing too much cologne jostling each other for the attention of women in tight dresses showing as much skin as possible without being completely naked.

The view outside Opal's picture window gave a glorious view of the city and above the skyline was a big fat full moon. The men would be extra horny tonight.

"Sorry, Nikki, you're on your own tonight. I've got a date."

"And you didn't tell me? Wait. Is he, you know, one of us?"

"Well, almost. He's not a werewolf. He's a werepanther."

"A cat? Whatever you do, do not fuck him. You hear me? Don't let him anywhere near your coochie."

"Excuse me?"

"Don't you know anything? Cats have spikes on their dicks. You ever wonder why girl cats scream bloody murder while mating? They got a spiked dick up in there and it hurts like hell."

"Markos is a werepanther. He's not some alley cat."

"A cat's a cat and the bigger the cat, the bigger the spikes."

"The doorbell's ringing. He's here. I got to go, Nikki. I'll talk at you later."

"Just remember what I told you about the spikes."

Opal hung up the phone and answered the door. Markos leaned against the doorway. He wore a tailored suit and great shoes.

"You clean up nice," Opal said.

"Thank you," Markos said. "Whatever you're cooking, it smells terrific."

"Then come on in and have some."

Opal moved to the side, but Markos didn't budge. Opal crossed her arms.

"I'm not going to feed you out in the hallway."

Markos waited another minute before sauntering into the apartment. He handed Opal a bottle of expensive wine and then without asking permission, he investigated every room. If it weren't for the fact that he was incredibly handsome and smelled fantastic, Opal would have ended the date right then and there.

She had made roasted vegetables and homemade bread. The steak was rare and bloody. The wine fit the meal perfectly. Opal was pleased to see Markos dig into his meal with gusto.

"I'm glad to see you're not one of those cats who are picky eaters," Opal said.

"I'm not entirely like a cat," Markos replied between bites. "Just like you're not always like a wolf. For instance, you didn't sniff my butt when you greeted me at the door."

Opal giggled. I only do that if you're lucky, she thought.

As the evening progressed, Opal found herself charmed by Markos. He helped with dishes. Except for when a pigeon landed outside on the kitchen windowsill and he couldn't stop staring at the bird until it flew away, Markos listened attentively to Opal and asked questions. At the same time, he did typical male things like stare at her tits, but then that was why she'd worn a low cut dress.

They finished the wine and Opal opened a bottle she had bought for the occasion. When it was empty, Markos made his move. Sitting on the couch, he leaned over and kissed her. It was a good kiss with the right amount of tongue and plenty of passion. Opal responded by wrapping her arms around his neck. His hands explored her body. When he began to snake a hand between her thighs, Opal grabbed his wrist and pulled it away.

"Before we go any further, there's some things we need to talk about," she said.

"Such as?"

"What do you call a girl who has a lot of sex?"

"Her name?"

"Good answer. Next, you're going to have to show me your real self."

"Only if you do the same."

"Deal."

Opal closed the drapes. She reached back and pulled down the zipper of her dress. Markos grinned as the dress fell to the floor. She wasn't wearing a bra and she quickly slipped off her panties. Markos carefully removed his suit. Stripping off his boxer shorts, it was Opal's turn to grin as she admired his semi-erect dick.

"Okay. Time for the moment of truth," Opal said.

"No, wait."

Markos pulled Opal to him. He leaned down and licked the dark red nipples on her firm brown breasts. He ran his hand down her side and reached back and squeezed her ass. His erection pressed against her belly. Opal felt a tingle in her pussy. She wrapped her fingers around his heavy balls and gently squeezed them.

"I don't want to mess up this lovely apartment," Markos said. "I noticed there's a park three blocks from here."

"I don't want to put my clothes back on. You got me too turned on. Let's just do it now."

"But you said you wanted to see the real me and I want to see the real you."

"I changed my mind. Let's do it human style this time. We can be the real us next time."

Markos kissed Opal. She liked it better than the first kiss.

"Please. Let's wait a little longer. Do you have access to the roof?"

Opal sighed. Why did he have to get her all worked up? Why did he tease her like this? Oh right, because he was a motherfucking cat.

Markos peeked out the door.

"Come on. The hallway's empty."

He hurried down the hall with Opal following close behind, admiring his muscular ass on the way. The door to the stairwell was next to the elevator. Just as they reached it, the elevator dinged and its doors began to slide open.

"Oh, shit!" Opal said. "Now what do we do?"

"We hurry the fuck up," Markos said.

He pushed the door open and they slipped inside. They climbed the stairs to the next floor and waited with their backs against the sooty cinder block wall.

"Do you think they saw us?" Opal whispered. Her heart was racing and her feet were cold.

"I don't think so," Markos replied.

A door below them opened, the sound echoing in the stairwell. Opal clutched Markos' arm. They held their breath as the sound of footsteps receded. Whoever had entered the stairwell was going down.

"Do you think they're looking for us?" Opal asked.

"No. It was a lower floor than the one we entered. I think it was just somebody who decided not to use the elevator."

Opal rested her head against Markos' shoulder.

"What do we do if someone catches us?"

"We transform and eat them."

Opal moved a step back and glared at Markos. "Really?"

Markos smiled slyly. "Hopefully, it won't come to that, but it's an option."

Opal rolled her eyes. "Come on. Let's go."

On the roof, they admired the night sky and felt the cool breeze on their bare skin.

"Now, we can show our true selves," Markos said, as black fur sprouted all over his body. His nose extended and became a snout. His ears inched to the top his head and reshaped into half moons. He expanded in width and height. A tail sprang from the base of his spine. Teeth and claws appeared as his eyes turned into yellow orbs.

Opal remembered Nikki's warning about male cats. Worry dogged her as she studied Markos' crotch to see if there was anything spiky down there. Only the pink tip protruded from his dick's furry pouch, so there was no way she'd know for sure unless he was fully erect.

She shook her head. Nikki didn't know anything about werepanthers. The spikes were probably an urban legend like giant alligators in the sewers. Opal knew damned good and well that only wererats lived in the sewers.

"It's your turn," Markos said.

Opal took four steps back and transformed. Her breasts receded as her chest expanded and produced white fur. Brown fur with streaks of black grew along the rest of her body. Her face stretched and her teeth became sharp and deadly. She became three feet taller.

"You're a beautiful woman," Markos said, "but you are a magnificent werewolf."

Opal swished her bushy tail with delight.

"I can smell the trees in the park," Opal said. "Going there is a good idea. I know a few secluded spots that will be perfect for us."

"Something tells me I'm not the first date you've taken to the park," Markos said.

"Does that bother you?"

"Not at all. Do you also know the best way to avoid people on the way there?"

Opal stood on the ledge.

"Follow me," she said.

Opal leapt to the rooftop of the adjoining building. She had barely landed when Markos touched down next to her.

"Oh, you think you're fast?" Opal said. "Let's see how fast."

She dashed across the rooftops and leaped over city streets, swiftly erasing the three city blocks between her apartment and the park. When she reached the apartment building across from the park's entrance, Markos was missing. She looked around frantically.

Opal had been sure that he was right behind her. She peered down into the park, but detected no movement. She sniffed the air and couldn't find his scent. She looked back the way she came. He wasn't lagging behind her.

"Shit!" Opal said. "Where the fuck did you go?"

Hoping that he was in the park waiting to brag how he'd beaten her, Opal climbed down the side of the apartment building, and once she was sure no one was around, sprinted across the street and into the park. She stayed off the trail and headed deep into the thicket of trees. She still couldn't pick up his scent, but the sounds of animals scurrying about mixed with the smell of pine and oak filled her with joy. In the woods, Opal felt as if she were shedding her human life and returning to her natural state as a wolf.

Without a single rustle of leaves or a branch snapping to warn her, Markos jumped out from behind a tree. He didn't hiss or show his claws. He just appeared out of nowhere. Opal yelped and stumbled backwards.

"What the fuck was that!" she shouted, lunging at him with her claws searching for his throat.

Markos grabbed her wrists and twisted her around. With his massive arms wrapped around her, he held her hands by her stomach.

"Sorry," Markos said. "Cat joke. Guess you have to be a cat to get it."

"This is the most fucked up date I have ever been on," Opal said. "Maybe panthers and wolves are too much like cats and dogs. Maybe we're not meant to be around each other."

Markos nuzzled Opal's neck. He began to purr, and his purring made his body throb, which Opal found soothing.

"I'm really sorry," Markos said. "Please give me another chance."

His crotch was pressed against Opal's ass and she could feel something hard poking her. She didn't know if it was the size of the hard-on or the purring that made it impossible for her to say no.

"One of the clearings I was telling you about is just through these trees," Opal said.

Markos released Opal's wrists and she led the way to a grassy clearing surrounded by tall trees. The tree limbs overhead blotted out the light from the full moon, which was perfect. They could see in the dark, but a passing human would have a hard time seeing them without a flashlight.

They rolled around on the bed of grass, exploring each other's body. Markos stuck his head between Opal's legs and licked her fur around her pussy.

"Here, let me help you with that," Opal said.

She brushed the fur aside to reveal her plump mound. Markos' tongue swirled around her pussy and poked between the folds until he located her clitoris. The rough texture of his tongue sent shivers of pleasure through her body. His steady purring added to the vibrations happening inside her.

Opal writhed on the ground. She yipped and growled happily. Her left leg shook furiously like it always did when she was happy. Markos' strong hands kneaded her ass cheeks and his tongue slithered in and out of her. Opal could feel the orgasm building up inside, hot and eager for release.

"I'm going to come," she panted.

Markos' responded by purring louder. Opal felt like her ovaries was on fire as she came. She bit her arm to keep from howling.

Once she stopped shaking, Markos lifted himself from between her legs. He licked his paw and rubbed it on his face.

She had more orgasms inside her, and she wanted Markos to mount her and fuck them out, but then she remembered the spikes. Maybe they weren't an urban legend. Maybe Nikki knew what she was talking about.

There was only one thing to do.

"Before we go any further, I need to find something out," Opal said.

"Is this one of those things you said we needed to talk about?" Marko asked.

Opal didn't answer. She grasped the furry sheath that housed Markos' dick. She'd had a lot of practice coaxing werewolf dicks out of hiding, though they often didn't need much coaxing. As she stroked the sheath, the pink tip popped out. It grew longer and longer until his eighteen inch werepanther dick was fully exposed.

She gently raked her claws up and down the full length of his shaft. Markos moaned. His dick was smooth and smelled of pure animal lust.

"No spikes," Opal whispered. "Not a single one."

"What?" Markos said.

Opal ran her tongue around the tip. She licked the full length and then brushed her snout against his furry balls. Markos' tail curled and twitched. Opal opened her jaws wide over the head of his dick and stuffed as much of it down her throat as she could without gagging. Markos rocked his hips as he fucked her mouth.

She could feel he was close and couldn't decide if she wanted him to come in her mouth or stop and fuck her pussy. Markos made the decision for her. He pulled out and turned her around. She was going to guide him into her, but he found his way in on his own.

Markos' dick slid easily into Opal's wet pussy. This was the moment they had both been waiting for, when they moved beyond the finesse of human like foreplay and into raw animal fucking. Markos grabbed her hips and pounded into her. Opal met his thrusts by bouncing her ass against his groin.

Soon, she felt her second orgasm building up inside her. She wasn't sure she'd be able to keep from howling this time. Her lust-baked brain didn't care if she did.

She was delicious inches away from coming when Markos sank his teeth into her shoulder. The pain wasn't bad. It added to her mounting excitement. But then a much more intense pain spread throughout her body and she almost passed out. Opal realized that Markos had bitten into her shoulder to keep her from bucking him off her. The pain originated inside her pussy.

"Spikes!" Opal screamed. "You lying bastard. You do have spikes."

She tried to pull away but that made the pain worse. His spikes anchored her to him. Opal gritted her teeth and dug her claws into the ground. She prayed he would come soon and release her from the horrible agony.

"Relax," Markos said. "Let the spikes do their magic."

"What does that mean?" Opal cried.

"My dick is spiked for your pleasure. Once the initial pain subsides, they stroke the walls of your vagina. Some of us think they induce ovulation, but I think they're there to give a female the best orgasm of her life."

Opal wanted to believe him, but it hurt so damn much. She felt like her womb was being gouged out with a rusty fork. She had clinched her pussy walls tightly on his dick, but she forced herself to relax.

It was if the spikes had been syringes of morphine, after the first painful prick, the drug entered her system. Tingly sensations spread from her clawed toes to the tip of her tongue. Markos began humping her again and the glorious feelings multiplied tenfold. Her pussy juices bubbled out and dripped down her legs. She heard a deafening noise and realized that she was howling at the top of her lungs.

Opal didn't have one tremendous orgasm; she had a series of explosions. She'd never come so much or so hard.

"I'm going to come," Markos announced.

"Yes, please!"

He arched his back and dug his claws into the top of her legs. Opal expected a cat's yowl, but

Markos was a panther. He roared as he came, his dick jerking with each spasm inside her.

Afterwards, they lay in the grass and panted. Opal ran her hand down Markos' spent dick, but the spikes had already retreated into the shaft.

"You control them?" she asked.

"The spikes? Yes. Otherwise, I never would have let you give me a blow job."

Opal let go of his dick and scratched the side of his face, enjoying the feel of his black fur. Markos purred contentedly. Her body felt completely satisfied, but in her heart she felt dread. She could never go back to werewolf dick. A panther's dick was spiked for her pleasure, but the spikes also acted as an anchor.

A NEW WAGER

Father Brewer stared at the empty space on the wall where the crucifix had been. A cross-shaped outline remained from where it had protected the paint from fading. After the crucifix flew off the wall for the fifth time, Gloria Orozco stopped trying to re-hang the symbol of her family's faith and put it in a kitchen drawer.

Gloria placed a bowl of hot soup on the table in front of Father Brewer. He wasn't hungry, but he was chilled to the bone and the rising steam provided a dollop of warmth. He stirred his spoon in the thick broth to encourage more steam.

During his time in the Orozco's apartment, the bags under Father Brewer's eyes had gotten heavier and the wrinkles in his dark brown skin had gotten deeper. His salt and pepper hair had grown more salty than peppery.

"How much longer?"

Gloria's son, Guillermo had taken a chair on the other side of the table. The nine-year-old boy's face was etched with worry.

"That thing in there thinks he's winning," Father Brewer said, pointing toward the bedroom. "But we have Jesus. With Jesus, you always have the winning hand."

"It's been two months. How much longer?"

Gloria smacked the back of her son's head.

"Guillermo," she scolded. "Don't talk that way to a priest."

Guillermo's father, Eduardo, joined them from the living room.

"The boy has a point, Gloria," he said. "We can't live like this."

Gloria glared at Eduardo.

"What do you suggest we do? Run away like everyone else in the apartment building?"

"Maybe we should. For Guillermo's sake."

"And leave Vilma behind? Leave our daughter to the devil?"

Father Brewer understood their frustration. They had escaped the evil of poverty and lawlessness in Mexico to come to this low rent apartment in Atlanta, Georgia only to become victim to a greater evil here. How could they not feel that the game of life had been rigged against them?

He stood, felt woozy, and grabbed the chair for support.

"Please, have faith. There is no time limit on how long an exorcism will take. I'm not giving Vilma a root canal. I'm trying to save her soul."

Eduardo and Gloria stared at the floor in shame, but Guillermo scowled at the priest.

"I'm sorry, Father," Eduardo said. "We're good Catholics. Vilma is a good girl. We go to church every Sunday. Why this is happening to us?"

"Evil feeds on the innocent," Father Brewer said. "Few of us are prepared to deal with this kind of situation. That's why I called the Archdiocese to send a priest with experience performing exorcisms."

"I thought that was supposed to be you," Guillermo said.

Like his sister, Guillermo had black hair, brown skin, and a round face. He reminded Father

Brewer of the boy in Miami. It had taken Father Brewer three weeks to cast out the demon inside him.

"I have experience," Father Brewer said. He looked at Gloria and Eduardo. "But I have never encountered anything like this before. This is either a very powerful demon or Satan himself."

A voice that sounded like it had been dug up from a deep watery grave shouted from the bedroom, "No need for flattery, Father Brewer! My legs are wide open and ready for your holy seed."

Gloria crossed herself. Eduardo put one hand on his forehead and the other on his hip. The temperature in the room dropped and they could see their breath.

"It's starting again," Guillermo said. He rushed to his mother and wrapped his arms around her waist.

Father Brewer couldn't wait any longer. He took a deep breath and walked toward the bedroom. He put his hand on the doorknob and quickly pulled it away. The brass was so cold it had stung his skin. The sound of cackling and heavy footsteps stomping came from inside the room. His fingers trembled as he reached for the knob again.

The doorbell rang.

As Eduardo went to answer the front door, Father Brewer whispered a prayer of thanks for the momentary delay. He hurried away from the bedroom door to see if his assistant had arrived.

Eduardo held the door open for the visitor. The setting sun was behind him making him appear as a dark figure outlined in red light.

He stepped into the hallway and Father got his first good look at the priest who'd been sent to assist him. His black clerical shirt strained to contain his wide chest and burly arms. The skin of his thick neck poured out of the top of his white collar. He had short unruly brown hair and a full beard. His brown eyes were so dark they were almost black. His skin was a light chestnut. Father Brewer tried to guess the priest's ethnic background, but he could have been anything from Latin American to Middle Eastern.

The priest shook Eduardo's hand and then grabbed Father Brewer's hand. He pumped it vigorously.

"You must be Father Brewer," he said. "I'm Father Jacob, but just call me Jacob."

Father Brewer couldn't place the priest's accent. The man might as well have grown up on the moon.

"Jacob?" Father Brewer said. He pulled his hand back and wiggled his fingers to get the circulation to return. "I was expecting Father McGuire."

"McGuire couldn't make it so the Archbishop called me in to take his place. He would have called to tell you about the substitution, but we felt that time was of the essence."

Gloria and Guillermo came to see the new priest. They craned their necks to look at his face.

"Would you like some soup?" Gloria asked.

"I would love some," Jacob said.

"You just said that time was of the essence," Father Brewer said, "and I couldn't agree more."

More cackling came from the bedroom followed by what sounded like a bull trying to knock down the wall.

"He's not going anywhere," Jacob said.

Jacob sat at the table and Father Brewer reluctantly sat opposite him. Eduardo and Guillermo joined them. Father and son watched Jacob's every move.

"Nice place you have here, Eduardo," Jacob said. "There's two bedrooms, right?"

"Si," said Eduardo. "How did you know my name? I never got a chance to tell you."

"They told me everything before I got here. Your daughter, Vilma, is fifteen. You weren't convinced she was possessed until her face turned green and the bed began to do the Mexican Hat Dance."

Eduardo gaped at the priest. Gloria placed a bowl and a spoon in front of Jacob. He scooped some of the broth into his mouth, sat back, and clapped his hands.

"That is the best pozole I've had in years!" he said. "Father Brewer, if you haven't already had some of this, you really owe it to yourself to try it."

The bowl Gloria had given Father Brewer was still on the table and had grown cold.

"I had some. It was good."

Jacob ate as if he were afraid someone was going to try and take his food away from him. Father Brewer's stomach churned with worry as he watched the large man slurping his soup. An exorcism was a highly specialized procedure. Only a handful of priests had the training to perform them. It seemed unlikely that the Archdiocese would be able to find a last minute replacement.

There was something about Jacob that didn't seem right to Father Brewer. Although he'd just met the man, Father Brewer would have bet a million dollars that Jacob wasn't really a priest.

A frightful realization came to Father Brewer. This charlatan wanted to capitalize on a tragic situation. Jacob, if that was his real name, didn't believe the girl in the next room was actually possessed by a vile demon. He was probably a reporter hoping to do an expose of the Catholic Church and its archaic belief that the Devil walked among us. As if Father Brewer's task wasn't perilous enough, this buffoon's meddling could doom them all.

"Before we begin, Jacob," Father Brewer said, "I'd like to call the Archbishop to let him know that you arrived safely and to give him a progress report."

Jacob tilted his bowl and swallowed the last of the pozole. He wiped his mouth with the back of his hand.

"If that will make you feel better then go right ahead," he said. "As for me, I'm going in."

Flustered, Father Brewer hurried after Jacob as he walked toward the bedroom.

"Don't you want to know what I've learned of the demon?" Father Brewer asked.

"Doesn't matter," Jacob said. "Whoever he is, he has to go."

"Where is your bible?"

"Didn't bring one."

"Do you want to use mine?"

"Don't need it."

Father Brewer got in front of Jacob and used his body to block the bedroom door.

"I can't allow you to go in there!" Father Brewer shouted.

Jacob stopped and grinned at the priest.

"What's taking so long, Father Brewer?" shouted the voice inside the bedroom. "You coward! You don't have the balls to face me."

Jacob leaned forward and whispered in Father Brewer's ear. An impatient banging on the wall drowned out Jacob's words, but what he said didn't matter. His whisper gave Father Brewer courage. Relief washed over him. He stepped aside and then followed Jacob into the bedroom.

Vilma sat upright in a double bed. Her arms stuck out because they were lashed to the headboard with ropes. Strips of leather secured her ankles to the bed frame. She wore a stained nightgown. Her skin was a lizard green and her irises were blood red. Her long black hair was a rat's nest littered with chunks of dried vomit.

The room smelled like a wild animal had been shitting sulfur. Cardboard and duct tape sealed the window and blocked the outside world. A dresser was crammed into a corner; it's drawers and their contents were strewn about the room. Chairs were stacked in the center of the room. A lamp sat undisturbed on a nightstand next to the bed.

Jacob and Father's Brewer's breath steamed as they approached the bed. Vilma stretched her mouth into a hideous grin and exposed her blackened teeth at the priests.

"I see you brought a friend," she said in the voice that was not her voice. "The more the merrier!"

The bed rattled violently. The lamp cast a shadow of the girl against the wall behind her. The shadow climbed the wall and became the shadow of a horned beast with wings.

Father Brewer pulled the vial of holy water he kept in his pocket and held up the gold cross he wore around his neck.

"In the Name of Jesus Christ, our God and Lord," he said. "We confidently undertake to repulse the attacks and deceits of the devil."

He opened the vial and squired a stream of holy water on Vilma. Smoke rose from where it touched her flesh and she howled in pain. The bed stopped moving and the beast shadow shrunk away from sight.

"You can't defeat me, Father Brewer!" Vilma moaned. "I will drag your soul to Hell."

The chairs in the center of the room swirled about as if caught in a hurricane. They started in a tight spiral and proceeded to spin closer and closer to the priests. Jacob held out his arm and one of the chairs flew into his large hand. He placed the chair next to the bed, sat down, and crossed his legs.

"Okay, enough theatrics, Stanley," Jacob said. "You must know why I'm here."

The other chairs stopped moving and then fell to the floor.

"You called him Stanley," Father Brewer said. "Why did you do that?"

"His real name is too difficult to say with human lips. Stanley is the best I can do."

Vilma studied Jacob, tilting her head from side to side like a curious dog.

"Jabbok?" she said. "What rock did they find you under?

"Detroit. I call myself Jacob now."

"Oh that is funny! Of course, you chose Jacob."

"Certainly you were expecting someone like me."

"Eventually. Why don't you let me finish up my business here and then I'll be glad to tear you limb from limb."

Father Brewer squirted holy water into Jacob's face, catching him off guard. He looked at the priest with surprise.

"You're a demon too!" Father Brewer said. "My faith in our Lord, Jesus Christ, is absolute. I will drive out both of you."

Jacob grabbed his stomach and guffawed.

"I'm sorry, Father Brewer," he said. "I shouldn't laugh. That was rude. I'm not a demon. And neither is Stanley."

"You will not deceive me with you wicked lies!"

"Doesn't matter if you believe me or not. You see Stanley and I are angels."

"Damn you, Jacob!" said Vilma. "I was almost done getting this good man to renew his faith and you go and tell him that Santa Claus isn't real."

Father Brewer picked up a fallen chair and set it on the opposite side of the bed from Jacob. He sat and regarded Jacob and Vilma warily.

"Kill me if you must, take my soul to Hades, but please let the girl go free. She is young and innocent. She has her whole life ahead of her."

"I've seen inside this girl, "Vilma said "Trust me, Father, she's not that innocent."

"Wow, Stanley," Jacob said. "You really did a number on this guy."

"If you hadn't shown up, he would have cast me out this time. Just like he did in Santa Cruz, Lima, Miami, and Rutland. It doesn't stick unless you make them fight for it."

"You're the same demon from all my exorcisms?" Father Brewer sputtered. "Did you torture those poor children just to get to me?"

The bed levitated three feet off the ground and landed with a loud bang.

"I wouldn't have had to if you weren't so easily tempted by gambling," said Vilma. "After each of those exorcisms, you returned to your church with renewed faith in Lord. You were as an inspiration to your flock and you scored me a lot of souls. But then, your faith would weaken and you'd start gambling again. What is it with you and Black Jack?"

Father Brewer slumped in his chair.

"Dear Lord, what have I done?"

"You have to admit, it's a good technique," Jacob said. "Who would suspect that an angel would pretend to be a demon so that priests can cast them out and believe that good drove away evil?"

"Are there no demons?"

"They exist. You're lucky none of your exorcisms involved them. A demon would have ripped your heart out. But you don't have to worry about possessions anymore. God and Satan have made a new wager in their constant contest over who can win the most souls. Used to be that direct contact was allowed, but the new wager rules state that angels and demons can only whisper suggestions into people's ears."

"Which has a much lower success rate," Vilma said. "And besides, whispering is boring and a complete waste of our potential."

Jacob stood and put his hands on his hips.

"That's not my concern," he said. "You knowingly broke the rules of the new wager. Leave this girl now and return to Heaven."

"Make me!"

Jacob's clothes disappeared and his skin turned gold. White wings sprouted from his muscular back and spread out majestically. A golden glow emanated from his powerful body like a lantern. Father Brewer stumbled out of his chair and pressed against the wall.

Jacob plunged his hands into Vilma. They entered her body without breaking the skin. The muscles in his arms bulged as he strained to pull Stanley out. As Stanley's head inched out of Vilma's stomach, she screamed in pain. Father Brewer felt like he was watching the girl give birth to a man. Father Brewer fell to his knees, clasped his hands in prayer, and recited Psalm 23.

"The Lord is my shepherd, I shall not want..."

Stanley stopped resisting his expulsion from Vilma and attacked Jacob. As the two golden angels wrestled, they smashed into furniture and their wings poked holes in the wall. Father Brewer crouched down beside the bed and watched in amazement. They moved so rapidly that he couldn't tell them apart. They blended together like molten gold.

"Help me," sobbed a small voice. "Please help me."

Father Brewer tore his attention away from the angels. In the mayhem, he had forgotten about Vilma. Her skin was no longer reptilian green and her eyes no longer resembled red-hot coals, but she was pale and her watery eyes beseeched him to save her.

When Stanley left her body, he freed her soul, but she was still strapped to the bed. She wiggled weakly against her restraints.

Father Brewer attacked the ropes that held her arms against the headboard. There were too many knots. He needed something sharp to cut through them. Just as he started looking for a possible tool, Vilma began shrieking.

"He's coming for me! He's coming for me!"

Jacob was on the floor holding his head and Stanley was rocketing toward Vilma. Stanley was at the foot of the bed, his hand inches away from the hysterical girl, when Jacob came up behind him. He wrapped his arms around Stanley, flapped his wings, and carried the two of them straight up. They broke through the ceiling and the next two floors before breaking through the roof.

Debris showered Father Brewer and Vilma. Minutes of eerie silence filled the room as the dust settled. Father Brewer rose up from the sea of broken boards, strips of insulation, and chunks of plaster. He had thrown himself over Vilma at the last moment to protect her. He checked her vital signs. Her face was caked with dust, but she was breathing.

Father Brewer climbed over the debris and peered up at the newly created skylight. The angels were like a gold star in the night sky.

During the battle, the bedroom door was reduced to splinters and the Orozco family cautiously peered into the room before entering. With her hands pressed against her cheeks, Gloria studied the aftermath.

"Did the demon do this?" she asked.

"We need to get Vilma out of here," Father Brewer said. "Do you have a knife?"

"No," Eduardo said. "Should I go get one?"

"Never mind. Get her legs free and I'll untie her arms."

Eduardo and Gloria went to work on the leather straps tied to Vilma's ankles. Guillermo clamored to the window. The cardboard covering was another casualty of the angel's wrestling match. The glass panes were broken adding to the currents of air flowing into the room.

"There's a bunch of people out there," Guillermo said. "They're pointing at us."

"Tell them to call the police and the fire department," Father Brewer said as he tugged at the stubborn knots.

"I was wrong. They're not pointing at us. They're pointing at the sky."

"It doesn't matter where the Hell they're pointing. We need help in here."

Guillermo see from his angle at the window what was holding the crowd's attention. He climbed over the debris to the center of the bedroom and looked at the sky through the hole left by the angels.

"Mama, Papa," Guillermo said, pointing at the hole, "Come see the golden star."

"We're busy right now," Gloria said.

"No, you've got to come now. This is important."

"More important than your sister's life?"

"Please Mama, come see."

Much to Father Brewer's surprise, Eduardo and Gloria joined Guillermo in the center of the room and looked to where he was pointing.

"He's right," Eduardo said. "It's a gold star. This is a sign. After our terrible trial, God has blessed us."

"The star is getting bigger," Gloria said. "What does that mean?"

"It's not getting bigger," Guillermo said. "It's getting closer."

The two angels plummeted through the hole they created and slammed through the floor, taking Eduardo, Gloria, and Guillermo with them. Father Brewer was trying to comprehend what had just happened when he heard a sharp cracking noise.

The rest of the bedroom floor gave way. For a brief moment the priest felt he was suspended in space and then the bed fell with him on top of it. The bed landed in the basement and the impact knocked

Father Brewer unconscious.

He opened his eyes in darkness. He was on his back. Every part of his body ached. He tried to cough out the dust in his lungs and was rewarded with shooting pains in his chest. Sirens wailed in the distance and people shouted.

A golden light floated toward him. When it got closer, Father Brewer recognized the angel.

"Jacob," Father Brewer said. "What happened?"

"My mission here is over," Jacob said. "It was a pleasure working with you."

The angel hovered above Father Brewer. His glowing body lit up the room so that Father Brewer could look around. They were in the basement of the apartment building. The center of the building had collapsed.

"Where is the Orozco family?" Father Brewer said.

"They're buried underneath us," Jacob said.

"Couldn't you save them?"

"They were good people. Their souls are in Heaven."

"That's not what I meant. Couldn't you save them from dying?"

"My mission was to cast out a rebel angel and that is what I did. Stanley has been sent back to Heaven where Lord will judge him."

"But what about the Orozco family? What about Vilma?"

"They were not part of my mission. As for Vilma, she's underneath you."

Father Brewer slid off the bed and saw the awful truth. When the bed dropped through the floor, he was standing over Vilma and her body broke his fall. Her lifeless eyes stared at him.

"What have I done?" he said.

"You saved her. She's in Heaven."

Father Brewer picked up a chunk of cement and threw it at Jacob. The angel flew to the side and the cement sailed past him and landed on a pile of rubble.

"What difference does it make?" Father Brewer said. "We're all just chips in a card game between God and Satan. My faith is meaningless. My entire life is a lie"

Jacob lowered himself next to Father Brewer. The priest beat the angel with his fists. Jacob's body was solid and hard. Father Brewer felt like he was hitting a brick wall.

"It's not part of my mission," Jacob said, but I'm going to do you a favor."

He whispered in Father Brewer's ear and the priest slipped into a deep sleep. Jacob lifted him like a child and gently placed him on the bed next to Vilma's body. He whispered in Father Brewer's ear again.

The firemen were shocked when they found Father Brewer alive in the rubble. It was a miracle that he had survived with only a few scratches. The building's destruction was blamed on a gas leak in an apartment on the third floor. It was a miracle that most of the residents were not in the apartment at the time of the explosion or there would have been more casualties.

A month later, Father Brewer met with the Archbishop in the Archbishop's office.

"Your exorcism reports are usually highly detailed," the Archbishop said, "but this one is full of holes. However, considering the circumstances, I'm not surprised. You went through quite an ordeal."

"Even now most of that day is a blur," Father Brewer said. "What I do remember clearly is that I fought a powerful demon. It took all of my faith and determination to cast him out of the Orozco girl."

"It's a tragedy that she died, but you saved her soul. This is a reminder of why we must be ever vigilant soldiers against evil."

Father Brewer held up his hand to disagree. He wasn't sure why he disagreed. His thoughts were jumbled and confused. Why would he have any reason to not believe that good must defeat evil? His fight with the demon was all the proof he needed. He put his hand down and stared at his lap.

"I have news that will make you happy," the Archbishop said. "Saint Paul of the Cross is having a casino night fundraiser next week. They need a dealer for the black jack table. I told them you were the best man for the job."

Father Brewer clutched his stomach and fought down the bile in his throat.

"Please tell them I'm sorry but they'll need to find someone else," he said. "Lately, the very thought of gambling makes me physically ill."